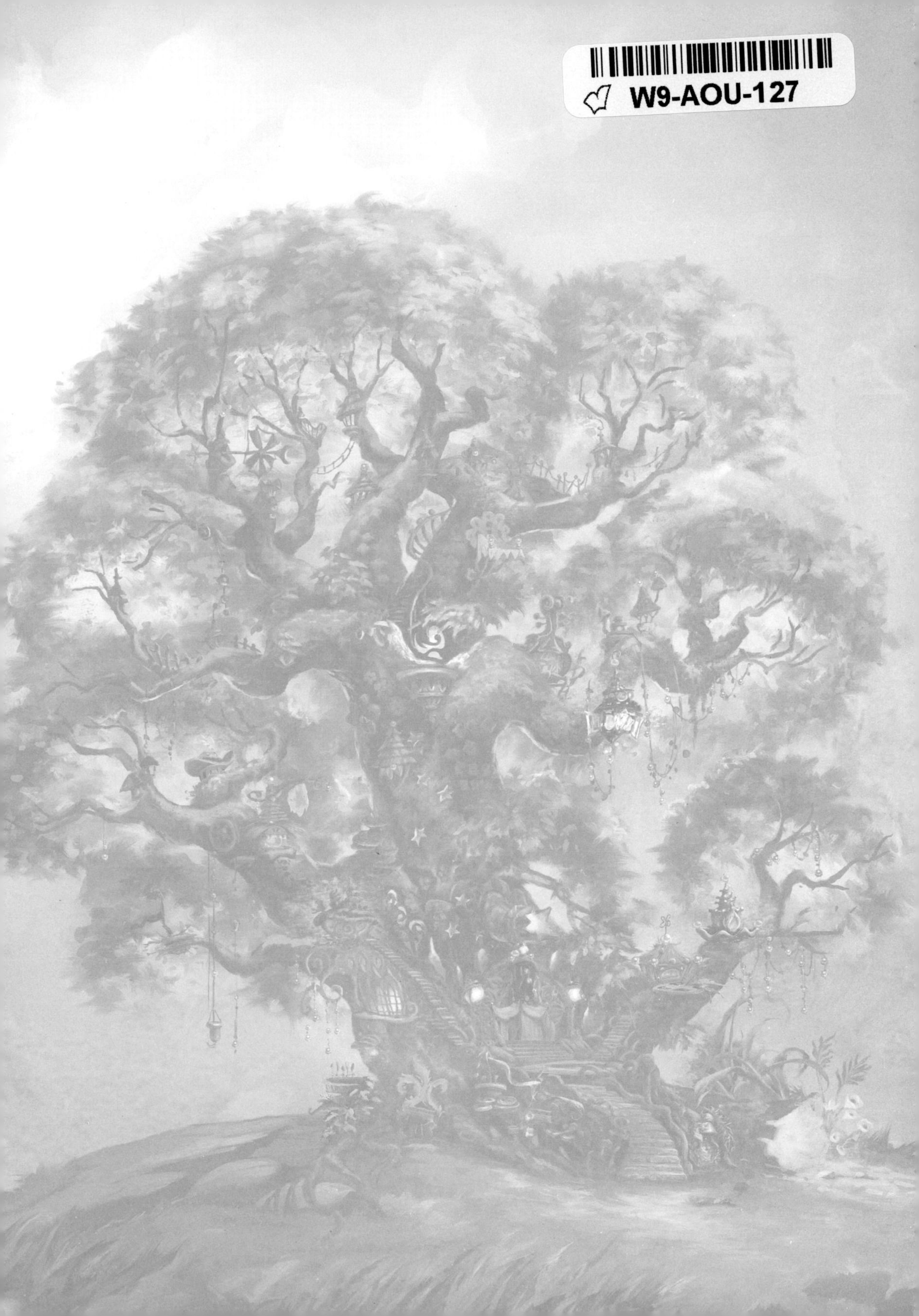

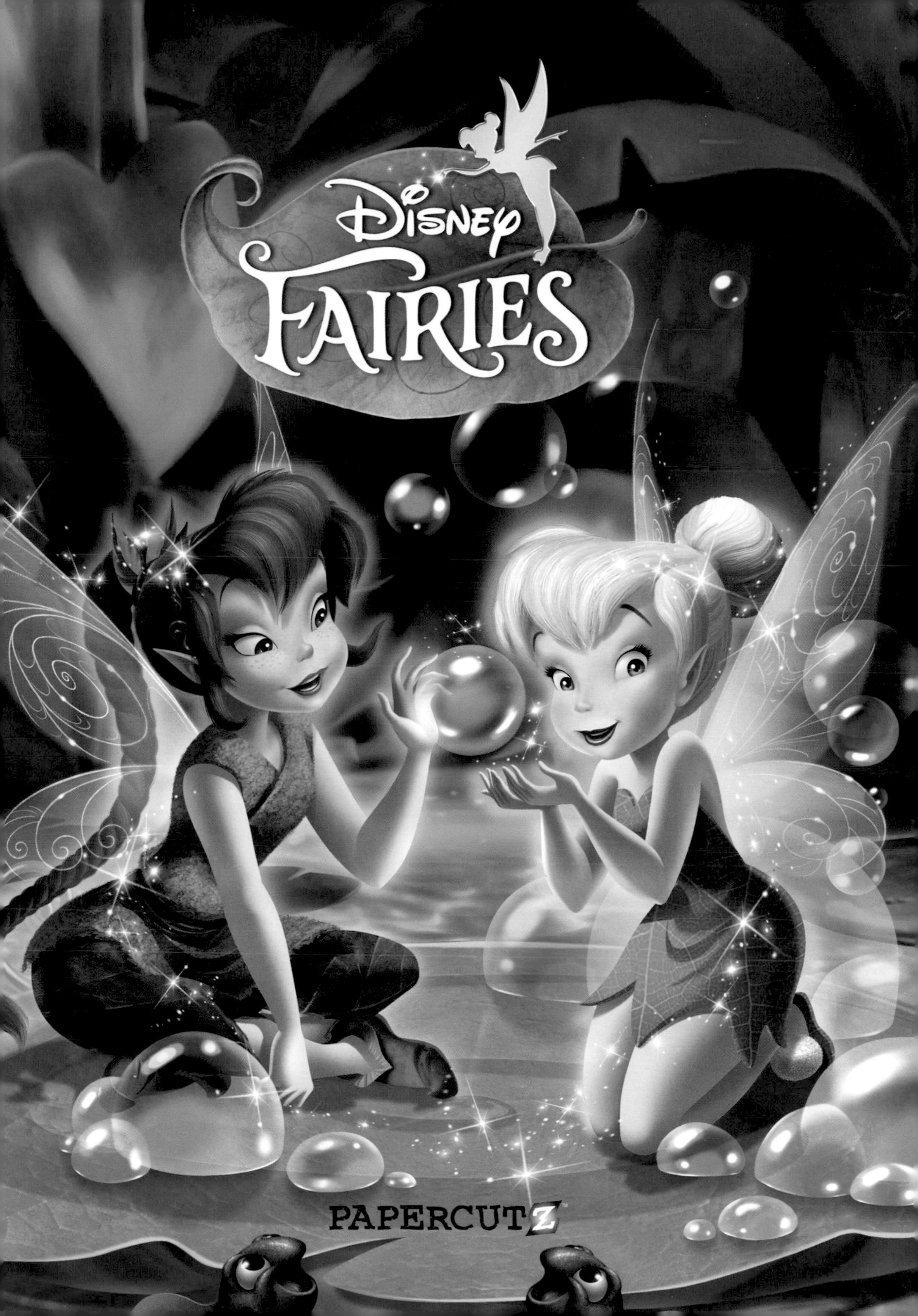
Disney
FAIRIES
PAPERCUTZ

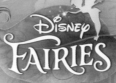

DISNEY FAIRIES

Graphic Novels Available from PAPERCUTZ

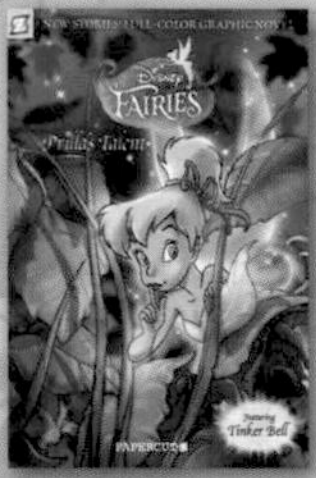

Graphic Novel #1
"Prilla's Talent"

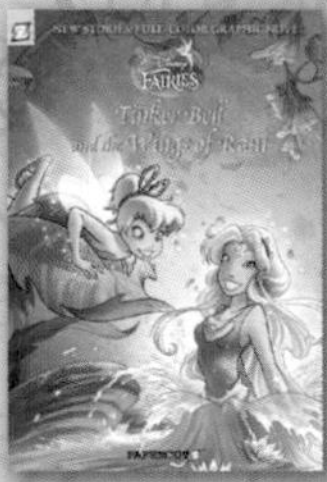

Graphic Novel #2
"Tinker Bell and the Wings of Rani"

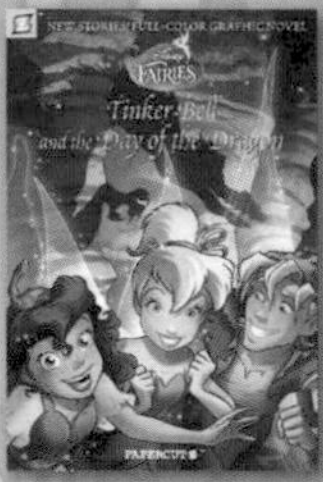

Graphic Novel #3
"Tinker Bell and the Day of the Dragon"

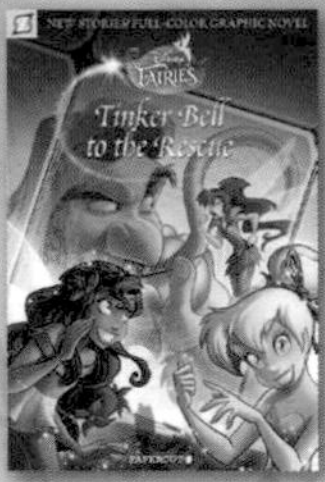

Graphic Novel #4
"Tinker Bell to the Rescue"

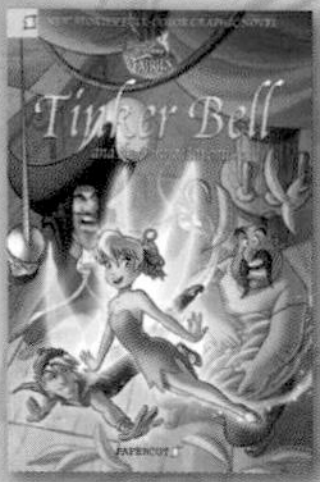

Graphic Novel #5
"Tinker Bell and the Pirate Adventure"

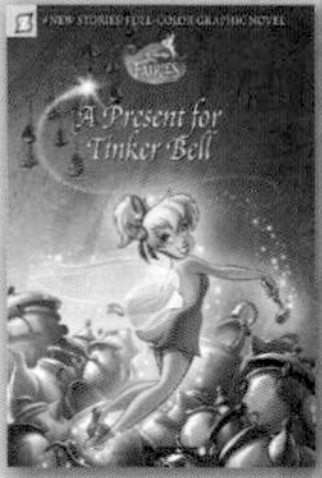

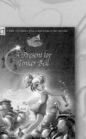

Graphic Novel #6
"A Present for Tinker Bell"

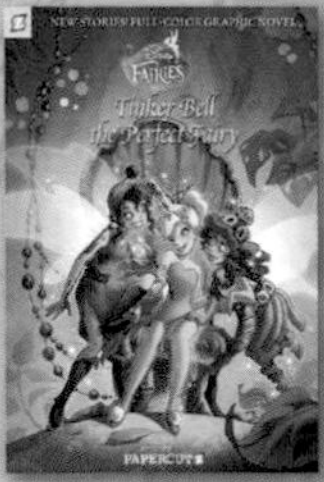

Graphic Novel #7
"Tinker Bell the Perfect Fairy"

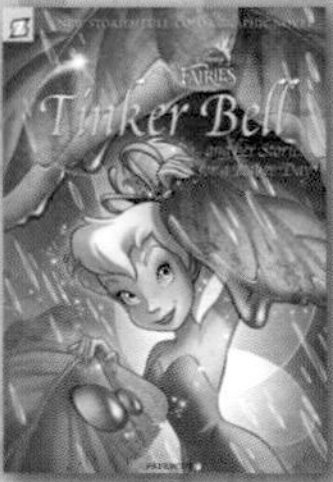

Graphic Novel #8
"Tinker Bell and her Stories for a Rainy Day"

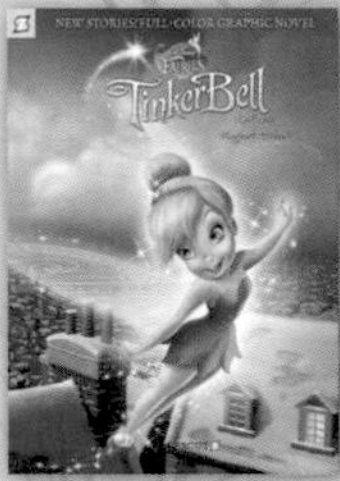

Graphic Novel #9
"Tinker Bell and her Magical Arrival"

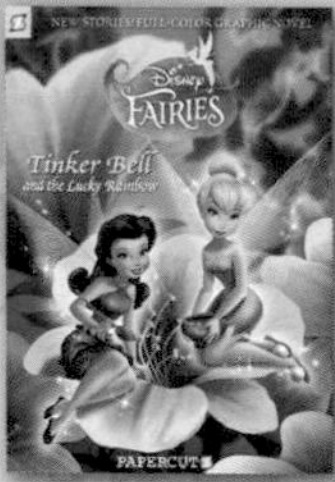

Graphic Novel #10
"Tinker Bell and the Lucky Rainbow"

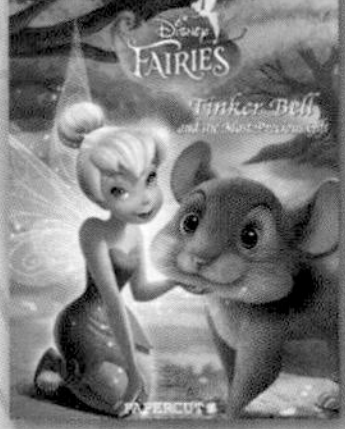

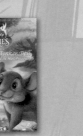

Graphic Novel #11
"Tinker Bell and the Most Precious Gift"

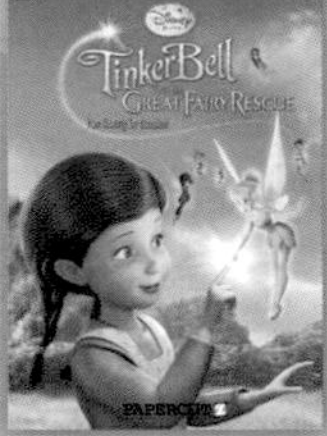

Tinker Bell and the Great Fairy Rescue

Coming Soon:

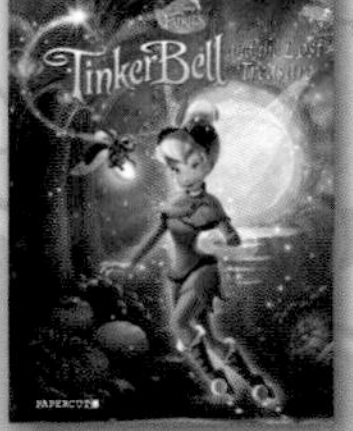

Graphic Novel #12
"Tinker Bell and the Lost Treasure"

DISNEY FAIRIES graphic novels are available in paperback for $7.99 each; in hardcover for $12.99 each except #5, $6.99PB, $10.99HC. #6-12 are $7.99PB $11.99HC. Tinker Bell and the Great Fairy rescue is $9.99 in hardcover only. Available at booksellers everywhere.

See more at www.papercutz.com

Or you can order from us: please add $4.00 for postage and handling for first book, and add $1.00 for each additional book. Please make check payable to NBM Publishing. Send to: Papercutz, 160 Broadway, Suite 700, East Wing, New York, NY 10038 or call 800 886 1223 (9-6 EST M-F) MC-Visa-Amex accepted.

#11 "Tinker Bell and the Most Precious Gift"

Contents

PAPERCUTZ™

NEW YORK

"Where There's a Dream, There's a Way"
Concept and Script: Carlo Panaro
Revised Dialogue: Cortney Faye Powell
Pencils: Manuela Razzi
Inks: Roberta Zanotta
Color: Studio Kawaii
Letters: Janice Chiang
Page 5 art:
Concept: Tea Orsi
Pencils and Inks: Sara Storino
Color: Andrea Cagol

"The Starlight Harvest"
Concept and Script: Tea Orsi
Revised Dialogue: Cortney Faye Powell
Pencils: Manuela Razzi
Inks: Marina Baggio
Color: Studio Kawaii
Letters: Janice Chiang
Page 18 Art:
Concept: Tea Orsi
Pencils and Inks: Sara Storino
Color: Andrea Cagol

"The Most Precious Gift"
Concept and Script: Carlo Panaro
Revised Dialogue: Cortney Faye Powell
Layout: Benedetta Barone
Pencils: Caterina Giogetti
Inks: Roberta Zanotta
Color: Studio Kawaii
Letters: Janice Chiang
Page 31 Art:
Concept: Tea Orsi
Pencils and Inks: Sara Storino
Color: Andrea Cagol

"A Prickly Problem"
Concept and Script: Tea Orsi
Revised Dialogue: Cortney Faye Powell
Art: Sara Storino
Color: Studio Kawaii
Letters: Janice Chiang
Page 44 Art:
Concept: Tea Orsi
Pencils and Inks: Sara Storino
Color: Andrea Cagol

"Rosetta's Night Out"
Concept and Script: Tea Orsi
Revised Dialogue: Jim Salicrup
Layout: Benedetta Barone
Pencils: Caterina Giogetti
Inks: Cristina Giorgilli
Color: Studio Kawaii
Letters: Janice Chiang

Production – Nelson Design Group, LLC
Special Thanks – Shiho Tilley
Associate Editor – Michael Petranek
Jim Salicrup
Editor-in-Chief

ISBN: 978-1-59707-394-3 paperback edition

ISBN: 978-1-59707-395-0 hardcover edition

Papercutz books may be purchased for business or promotional use. For information on bulk purchases please contact Macmillan Corporate and Premium Sales Department at (800) 221-7945 x5442.

Printed in China
March 2013 by Asia One Printing LTD
13/F Asia One Tower
8 Fung Yip St., Chaiwan
Hong Kong

Distributed by Macmillan

First Papercutz Printing

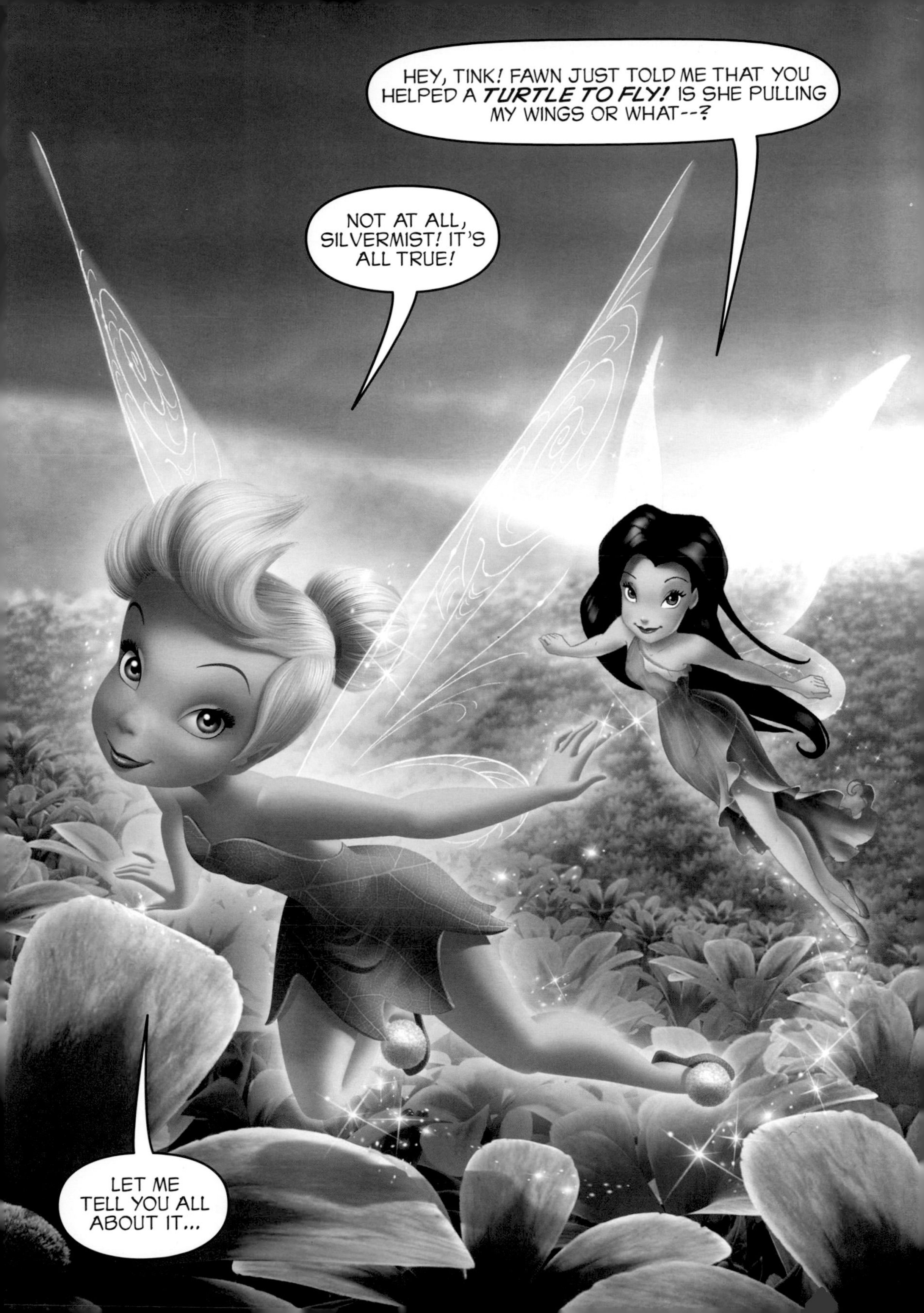
HEY, TINK! FAWN JUST TOLD ME THAT YOU HELPED A TURTLE TO FLY! IS SHE PULLING MY WINGS OR WHAT--?
NOT AT ALL, SILVERMIST! IT'S ALL TRUE!
LET ME TELL YOU ALL ABOUT IT...

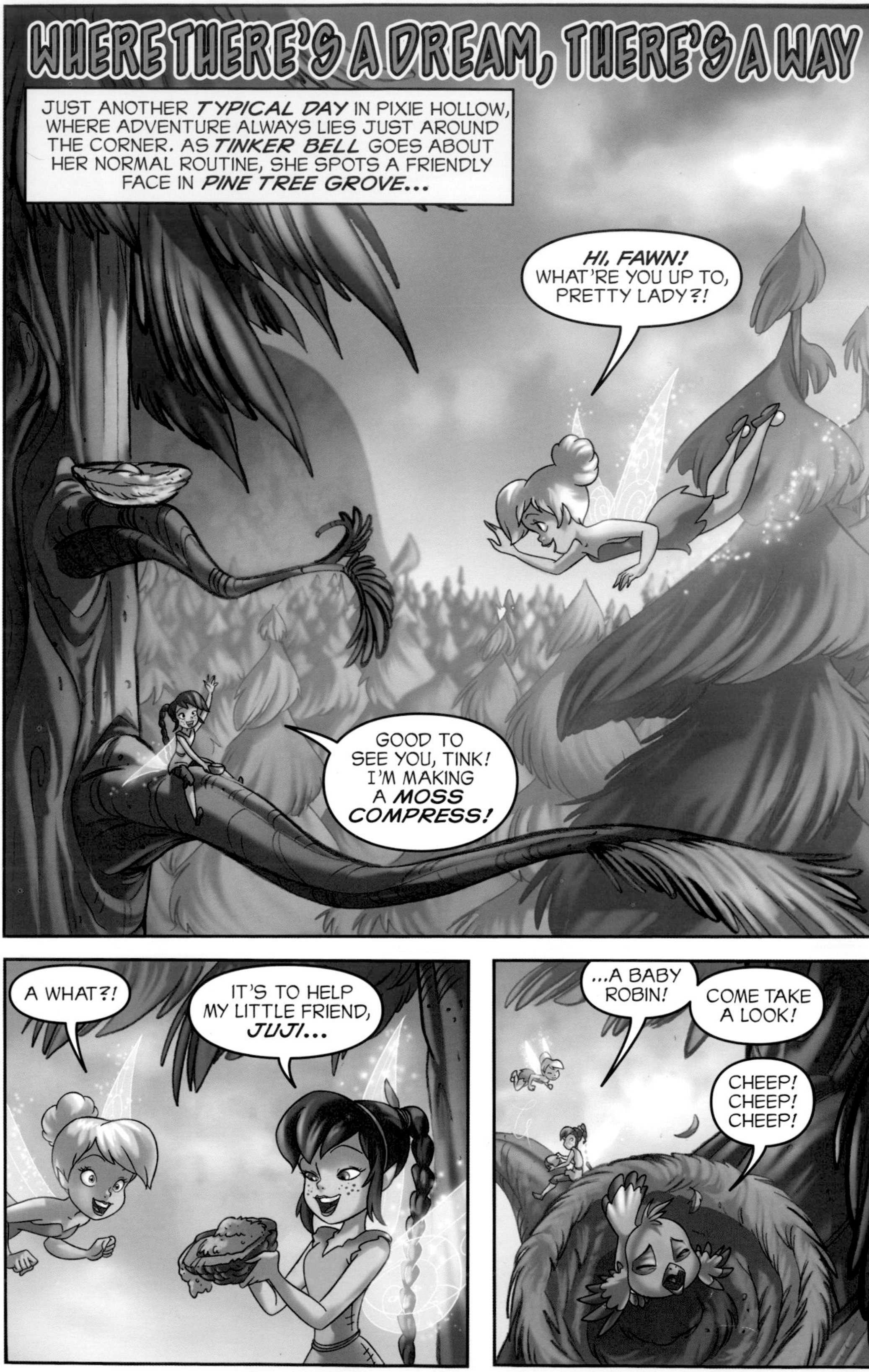
WHERE THERE'S A DREAM, THERE'S A WAY
JUST ANOTHER TYPICAL DAY IN PIXIE HOLLOW, WHERE ADVENTURE ALWAYS LIES JUST AROUND THE CORNER. AS TINKER BELL GOES ABOUT HER NORMAL ROUTINE, SHE SPOTS A FRIENDLY FACE IN PINE TREE GROVE...
HI, FAWN! WHAT'RE YOU UP TO, PRETTY LADY?!
GOOD TO SEE YOU, TINK! I'M MAKING A MOSS COMPRESS!
A WHAT?!
IT'S TO HELP MY LITTLE FRIEND, JUJI...
...A BABY ROBIN!
COME TAKE A LOOK!
CHEEP! CHEEP! CHEEP!

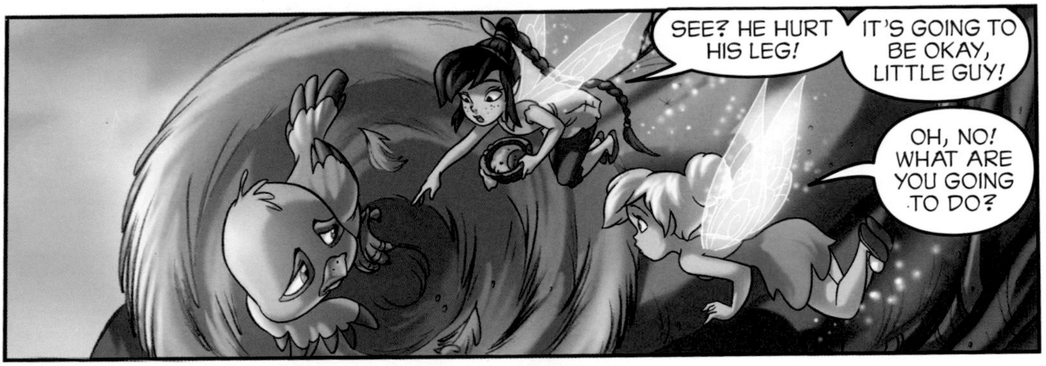
SEE? HE HURT HIS LEG!
IT'S GOING TO BE OKAY, LITTLE GUY!
OH, NO! WHAT ARE YOU GOING TO DO?

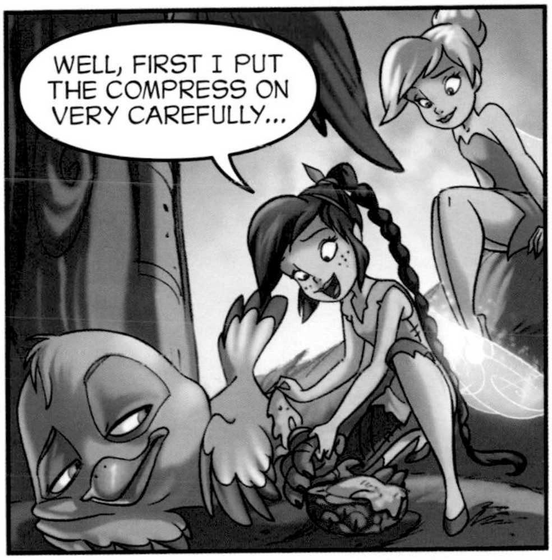
WELL, FIRST I PUT THE COMPRESS ON VERY CAREFULLY...

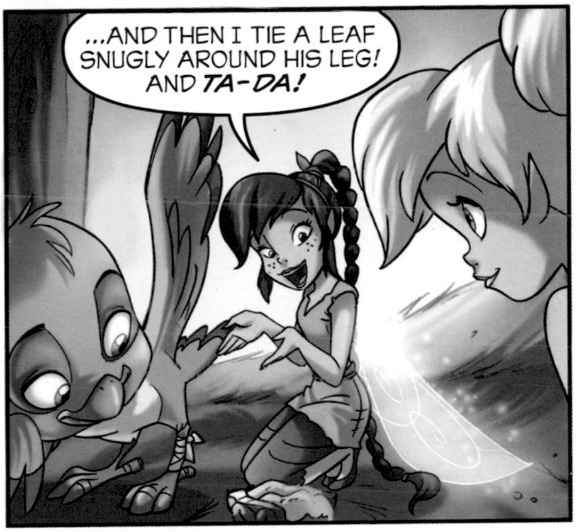
...AND THEN I TIE A LEAF SNUGLY AROUND HIS LEG! AND TA-DA!

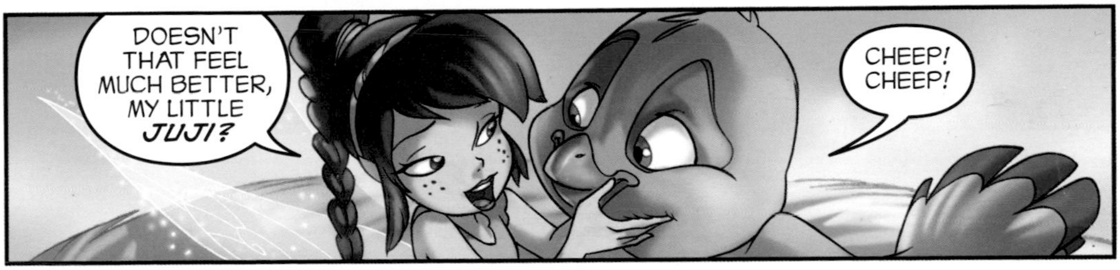
DOESN'T THAT FEEL MUCH BETTER, MY LITTLE JUJI?
CHEEP! CHEEP!

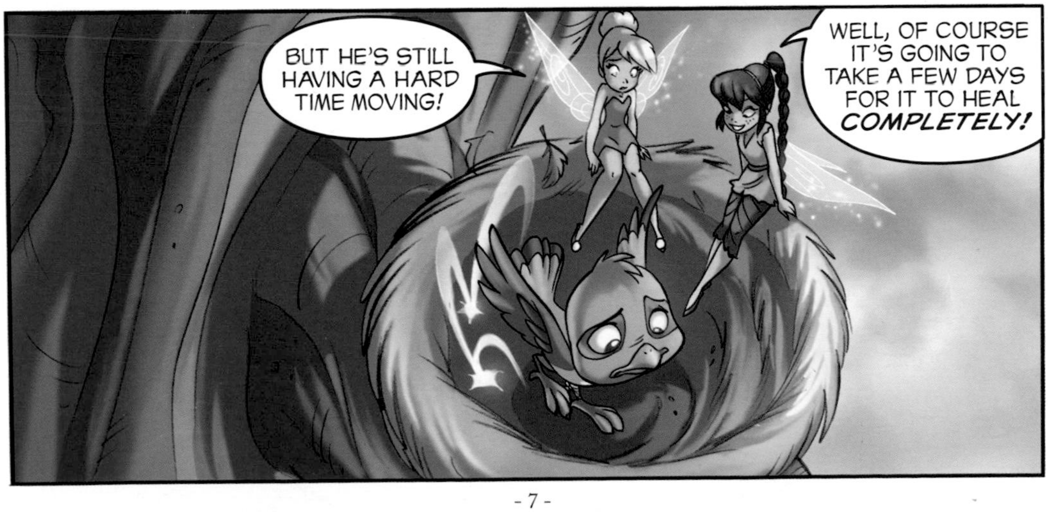
BUT HE'S STILL HAVING A HARD TIME MOVING!
WELL, OF COURSE IT'S GOING TO TAKE A FEW DAYS FOR IT TO HEAL COMPLETELY!

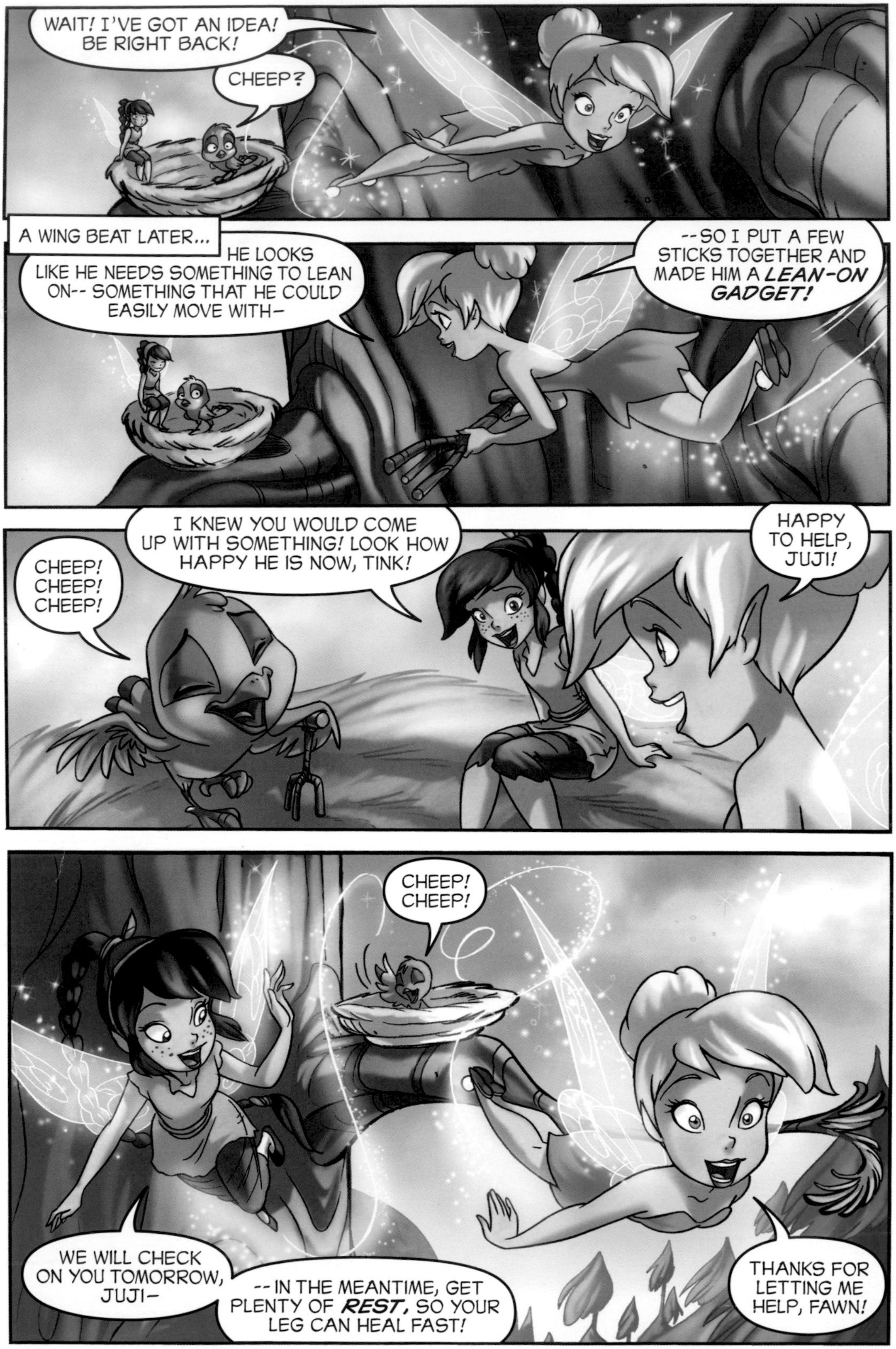
WAIT! I'VE GOT AN IDEA! BE RIGHT BACK!
CHEEP?
A WING BEAT LATER...
HE LOOKS LIKE HE NEEDS SOMETHING TO LEAN ON-- SOMETHING THAT HE COULD EASILY MOVE WITH–
--SO I PUT A FEW STICKS TOGETHER AND MADE HIM A LEAN-ON GADGET!
CHEEP! CHEEP! CHEEP!
I KNEW YOU WOULD COME UP WITH SOMETHING! LOOK HOW HAPPY HE IS NOW, TINK!
HAPPY TO HELP, JUJI!
CHEEP! CHEEP!
WE WILL CHECK ON YOU TOMORROW, JUJI–
--IN THE MEANTIME, GET PLENTY OF REST, SO YOUR LEG CAN HEAL FAST!
THANKS FOR LETTING ME HELP, FAWN!

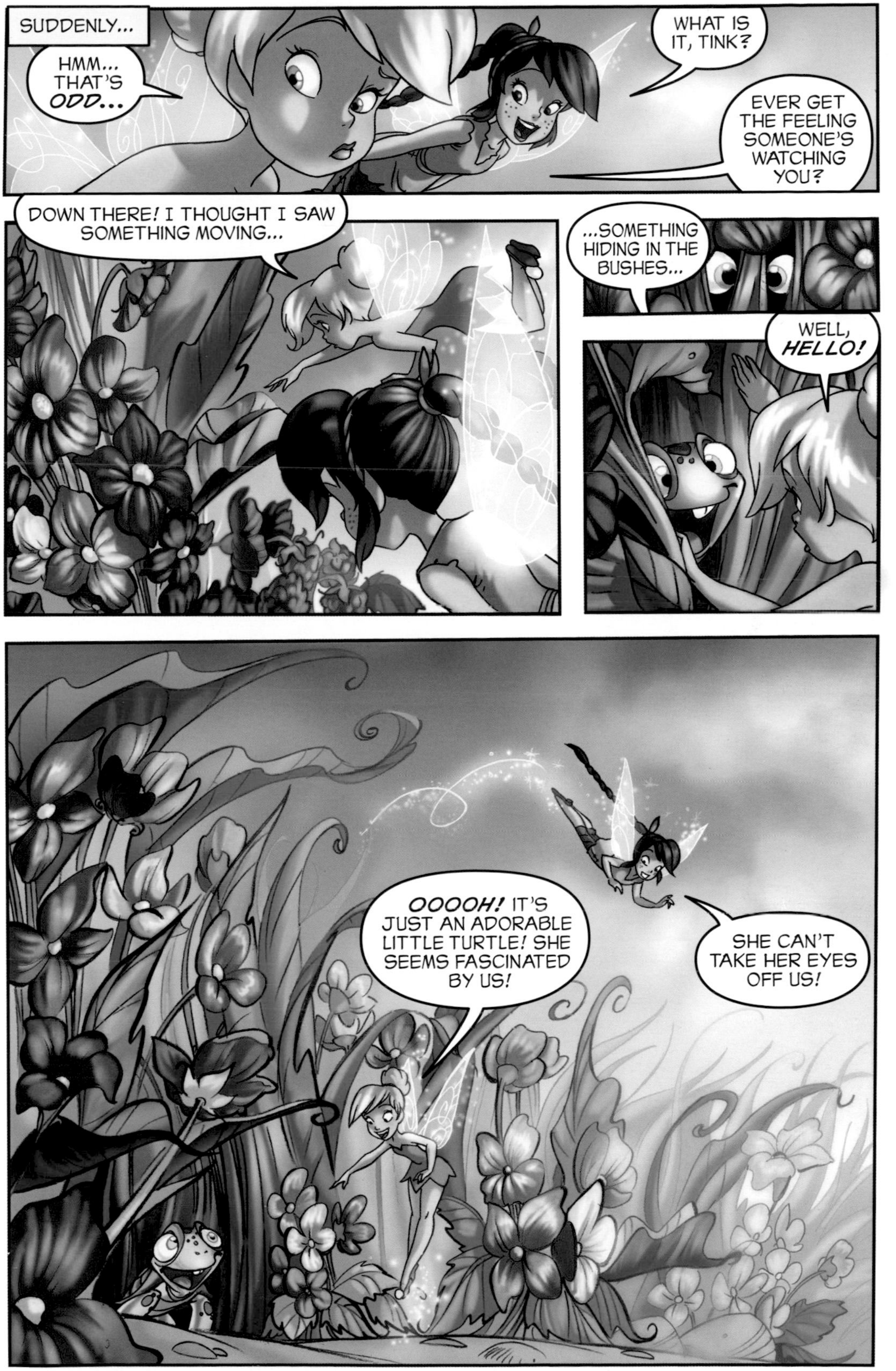
SUDDENLY...
HMM... THAT'S ODD...
WHAT IS IT, TINK?
EVER GET THE FEELING SOMEONE'S WATCHING YOU?
DOWN THERE! I THOUGHT I SAW SOMETHING MOVING...
...SOMETHING HIDING IN THE BUSHES...
WELL, HELLO!
OOOOH! IT'S JUST AN ADORABLE LITTLE TURTLE! SHE SEEMS FASCINATED BY US!
SHE CAN'T TAKE HER EYES OFF US!

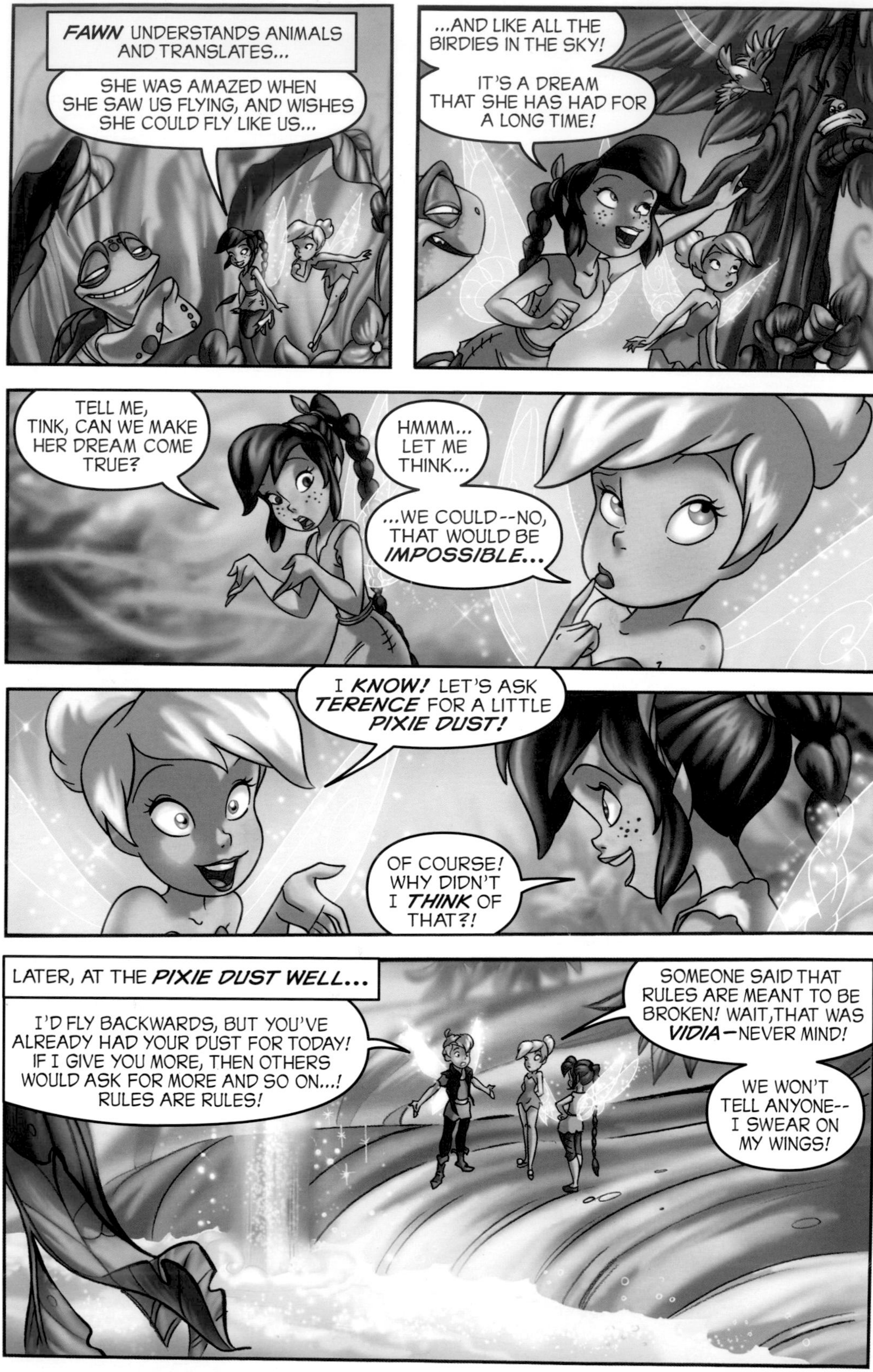
FAWN UNDERSTANDS ANIMALS AND TRANSLATES...
SHE WAS AMAZED WHEN SHE SAW US FLYING, AND WISHES SHE COULD FLY LIKE US...
...AND LIKE ALL THE BIRDIES IN THE SKY!
IT'S A DREAM THAT SHE HAS HAD FOR A LONG TIME!
TELL ME, TINK, CAN WE MAKE HER DREAM COME TRUE?
HMMM... LET ME THINK...
...WE COULD--NO, THAT WOULD BE IMPOSSIBLE...
I KNOW! LET'S ASK TERENCE FOR A LITTLE PIXIE DUST!
OF COURSE! WHY DIDN'T I THINK OF THAT?!
LATER, AT THE PIXIE DUST WELL...
I'D FLY BACKWARDS, BUT YOU'VE ALREADY HAD YOUR DUST FOR TODAY! IF I GIVE YOU MORE, THEN OTHERS WOULD ASK FOR MORE AND SO ON...! RULES ARE RULES!
SOMEONE SAID THAT RULES ARE MEANT TO BE BROKEN! WAIT, THAT WAS VIDIA—NEVER MIND!
WE WON'T TELL ANYONE-- I SWEAR ON MY WINGS!

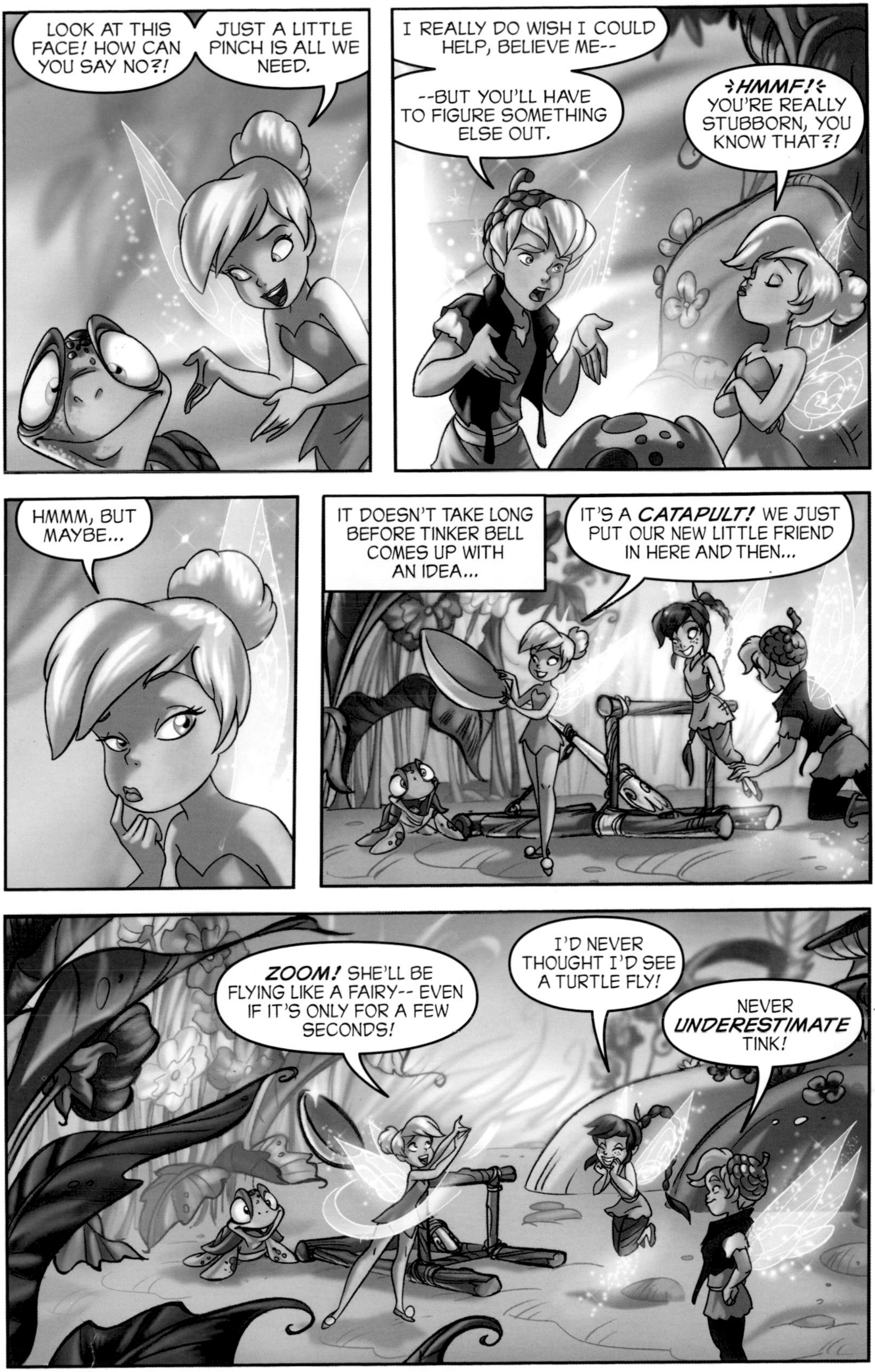

LOOK AT THIS FACE! HOW CAN YOU SAY NO?!
JUST A LITTLE PINCH IS ALL WE NEED.
I REALLY DO WISH I COULD HELP, BELIEVE ME--
--BUT YOU'LL HAVE TO FIGURE SOMETHING ELSE OUT.
HMMF! YOU'RE REALLY STUBBORN, YOU KNOW THAT?!
HMMM, BUT MAYBE...
IT DOESN'T TAKE LONG BEFORE TINKER BELL COMES UP WITH AN IDEA...
IT'S A CATAPULT! WE JUST PUT OUR NEW LITTLE FRIEND IN HERE AND THEN...
ZOOM! SHE'LL BE FLYING LIKE A FAIRY-- EVEN IF IT'S ONLY FOR A FEW SECONDS!
I'D NEVER THOUGHT I'D SEE A TURTLE FLY!
NEVER UNDERESTIMATE TINK!

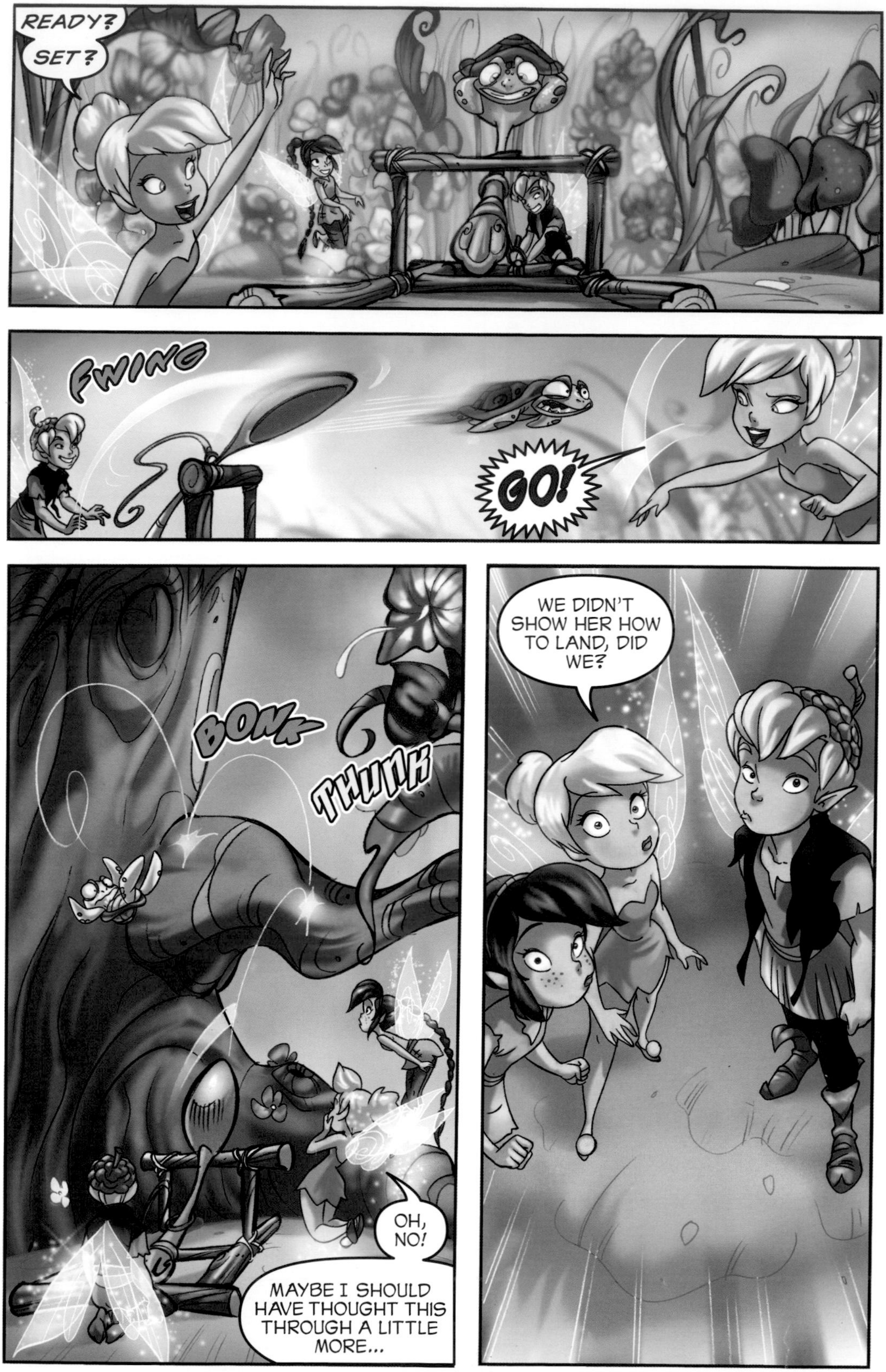
READY?
SET?
FWING
GO!
BONK
THUNK
OH, NO!
MAYBE I SHOULD HAVE THOUGHT THIS THROUGH A LITTLE MORE...
WE DIDN'T SHOW HER HOW TO LAND, DID WE?

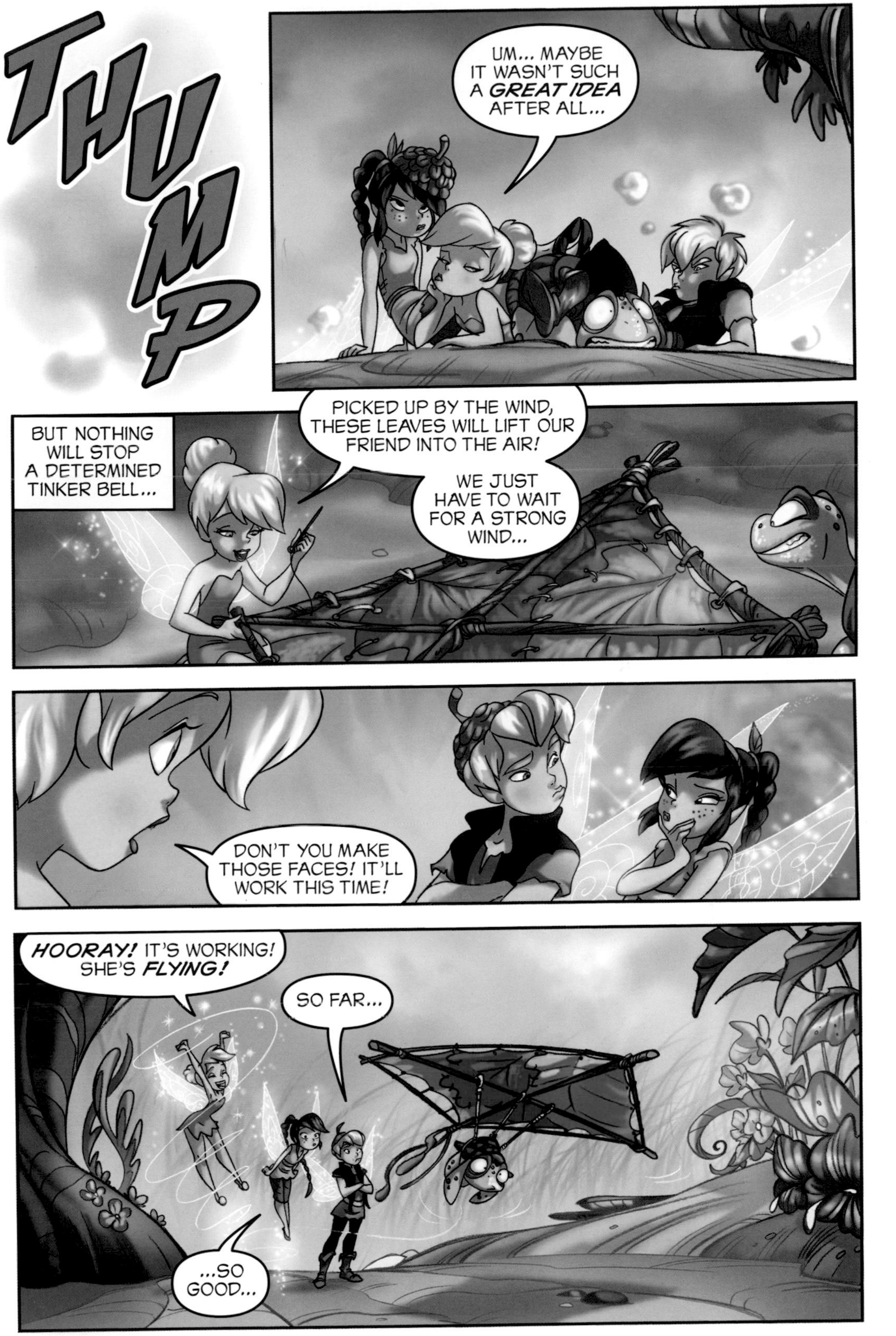
THUMP
UM... MAYBE IT WASN'T SUCH A GREAT IDEA AFTER ALL...
BUT NOTHING WILL STOP A DETERMINED TINKER BELL...
PICKED UP BY THE WIND, THESE LEAVES WILL LIFT OUR FRIEND INTO THE AIR!
WE JUST HAVE TO WAIT FOR A STRONG WIND...
DON'T YOU MAKE THOSE FACES! IT'LL WORK THIS TIME!
HOORAY! IT'S WORKING! SHE'S FLYING!
SO FAR...
...SO GOOD...

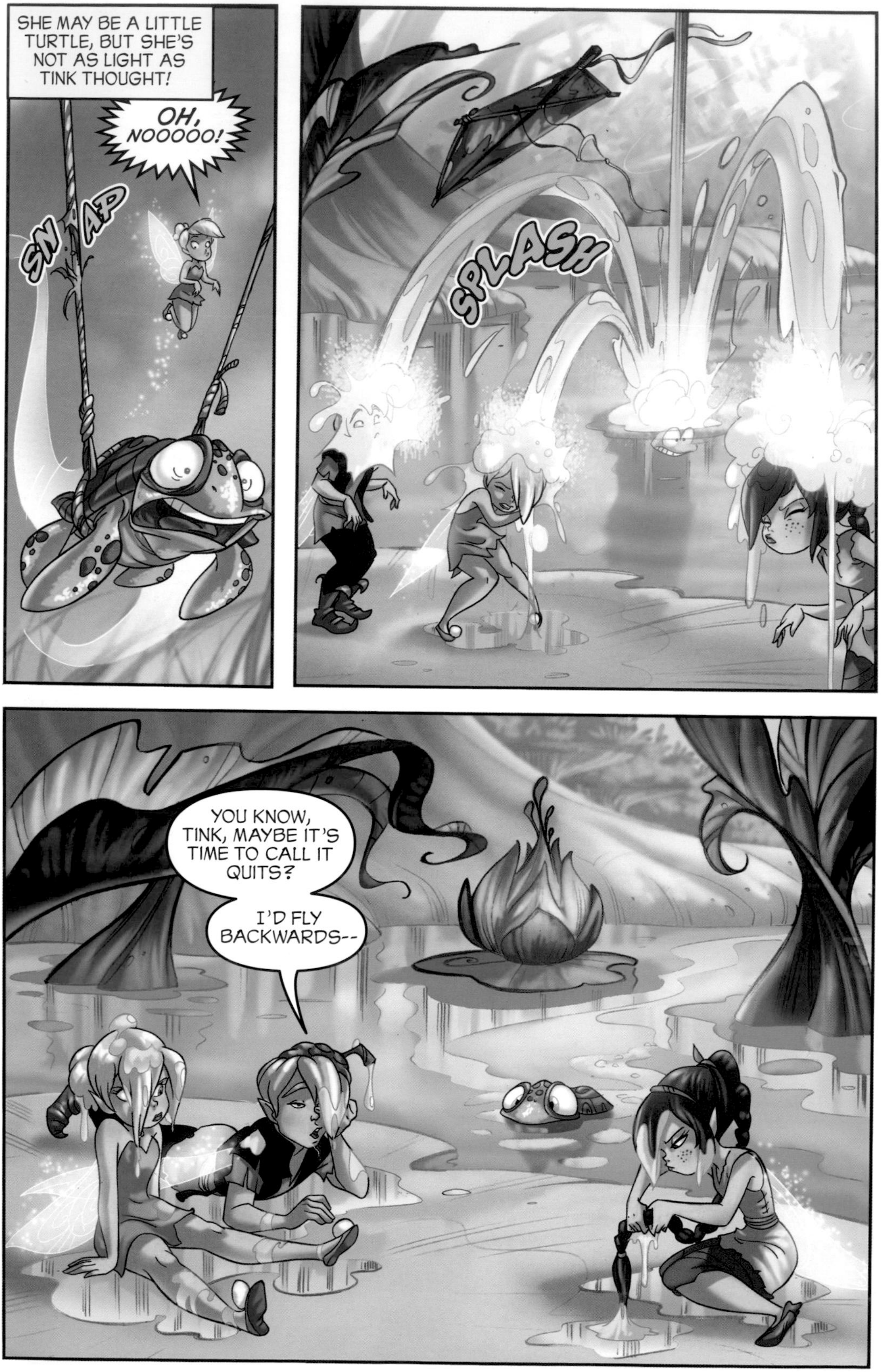
SHE MAY BE A LITTLE TURTLE, BUT SHE'S NOT AS LIGHT AS TINK THOUGHT!
OH, NOOOOO!
SNAP
SPLASH
YOU KNOW, TINK, MAYBE IT'S TIME TO CALL IT QUITS?
I'D FLY BACKWARDS--

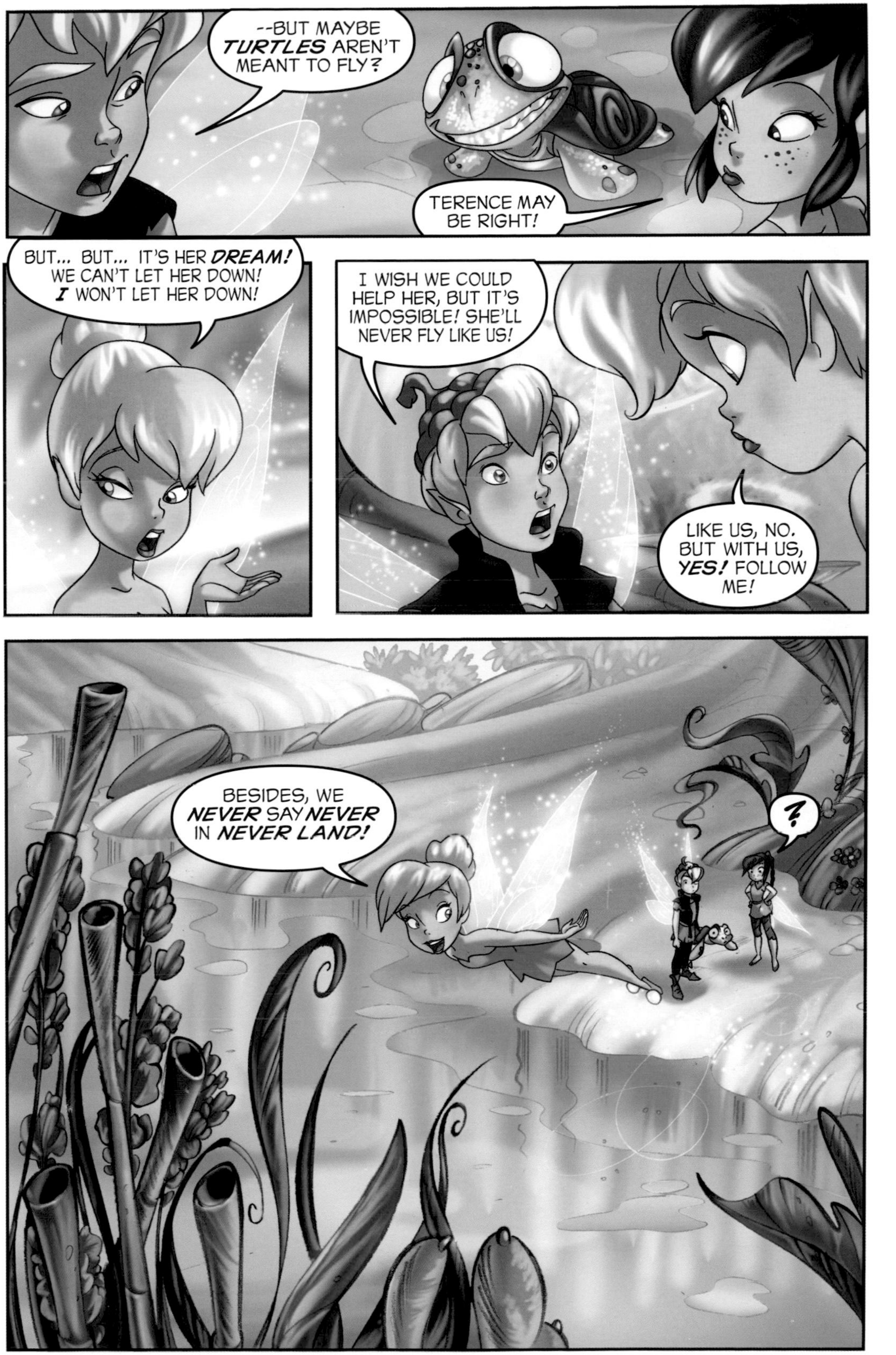
--BUT MAYBE TURTLES AREN'T MEANT TO FLY?
TERENCE MAY BE RIGHT!
BUT... BUT... IT'S HER DREAM! WE CAN'T LET HER DOWN! I WON'T LET HER DOWN!
I WISH WE COULD HELP HER, BUT IT'S IMPOSSIBLE! SHE'LL NEVER FLY LIKE US!
LIKE US, NO. BUT WITH US, YES! FOLLOW ME!
BESIDES, WE NEVER SAY NEVER IN NEVER LAND!
?

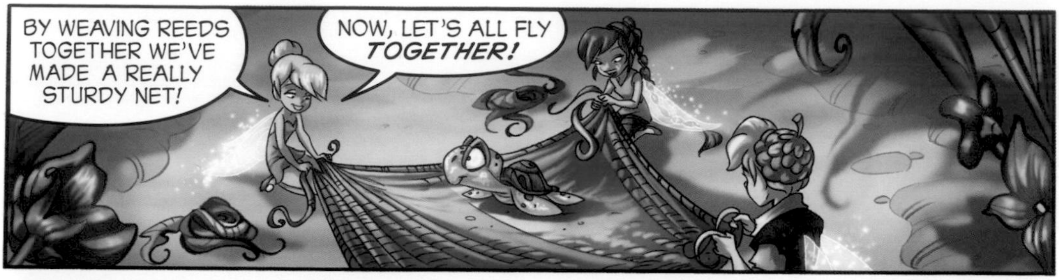
BY WEAVING REEDS TOGETHER WE'VE MADE A REALLY STURDY NET!
NOW, LET'S ALL FLY *TOGETHER!*

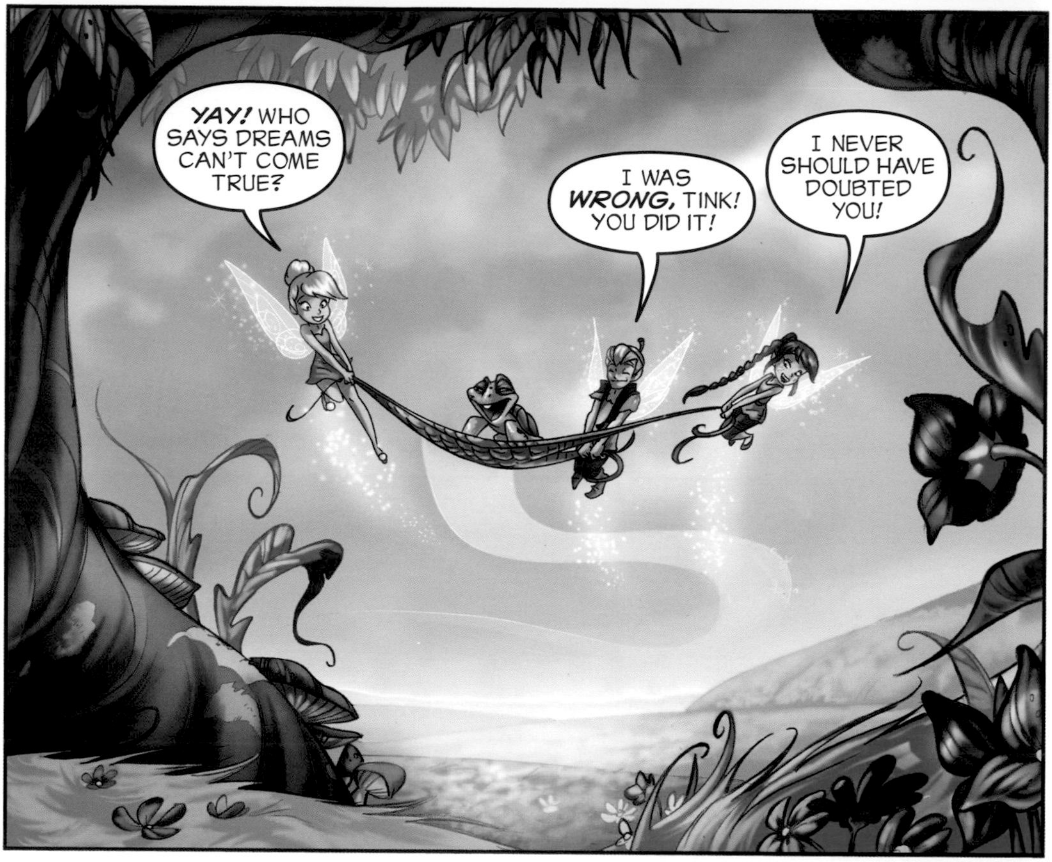
YAY! WHO SAYS DREAMS CAN'T COME TRUE?
I WAS *WRONG,* TINK! YOU DID IT!
I NEVER SHOULD HAVE DOUBTED YOU!

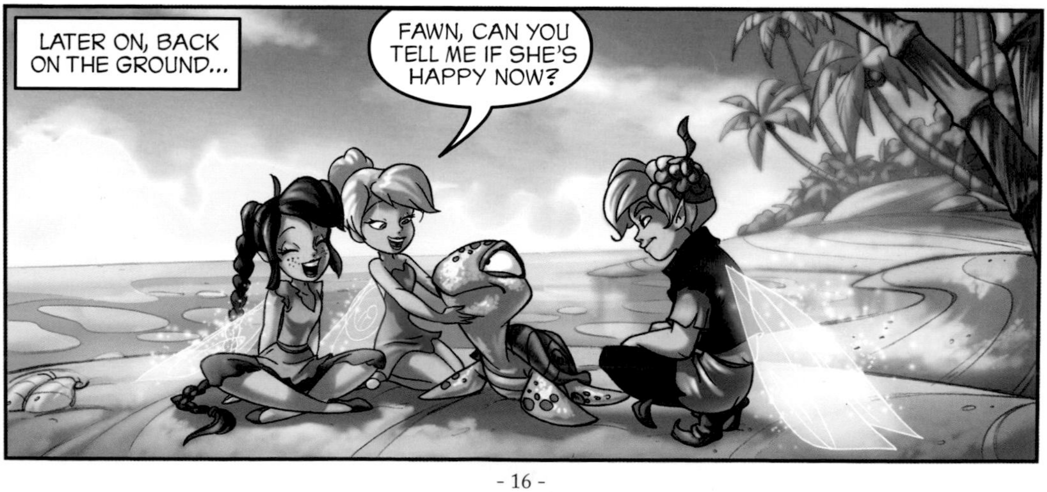
LATER ON, BACK ON THE GROUND...
FAWN, CAN YOU TELL ME IF SHE'S HAPPY NOW?

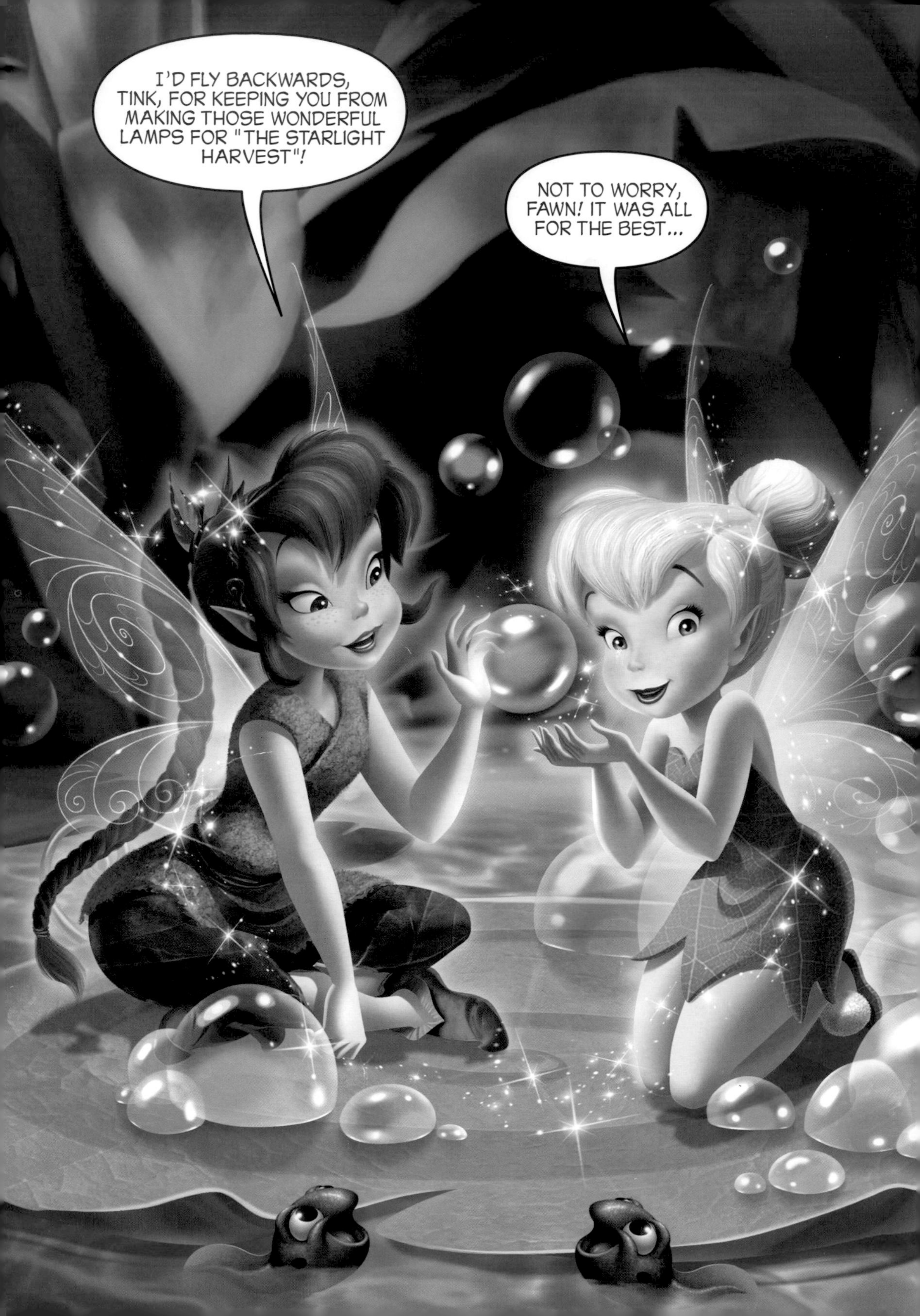
I'D FLY BACKWARDS, TINK, FOR KEEPING YOU FROM MAKING THOSE WONDERFUL LAMPS FOR "THE STARLIGHT HARVEST"!
NOT TO WORRY, FAWN! IT WAS ALL FOR THE BEST...

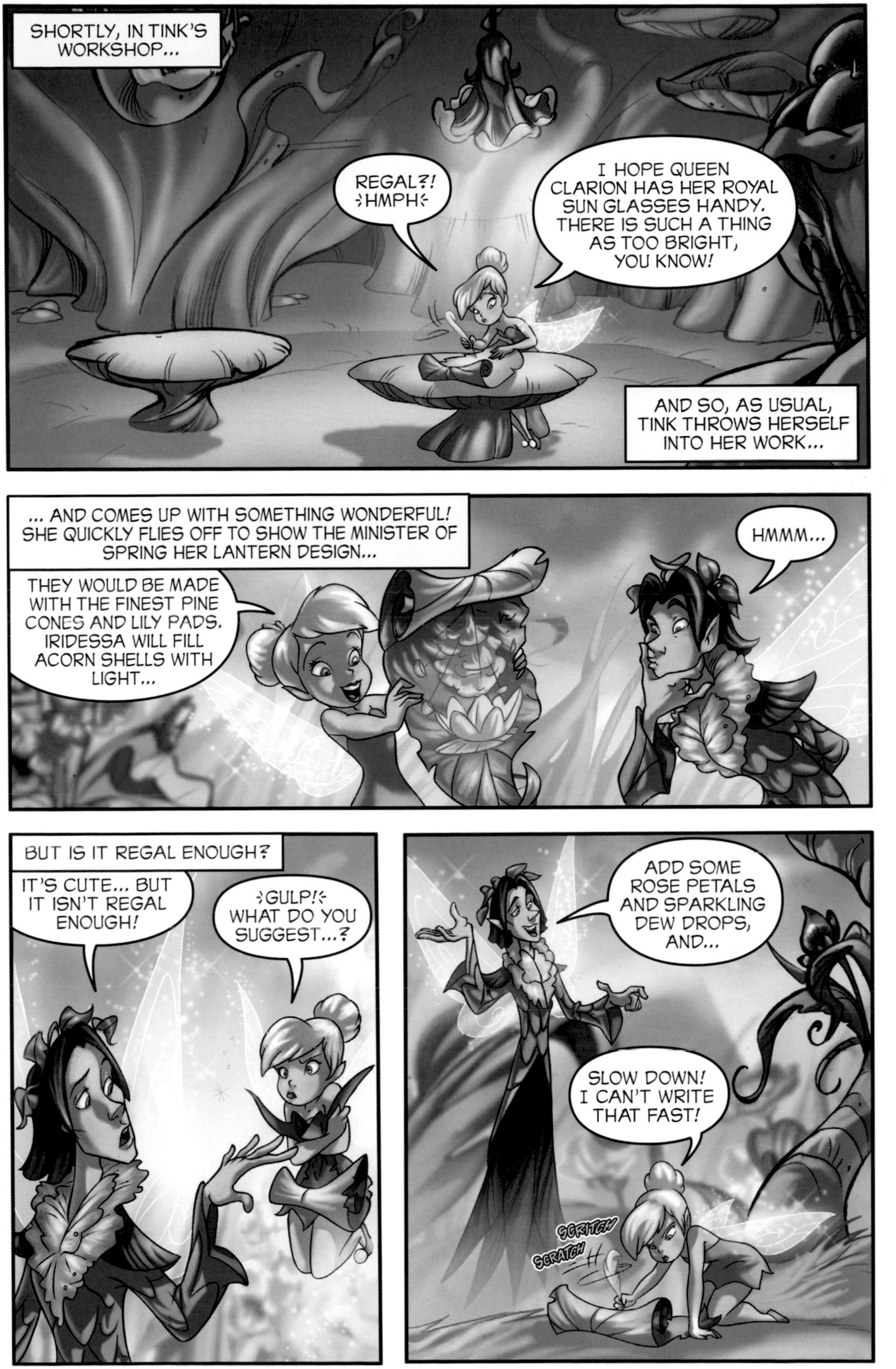
SHORTLY, IN TINK'S WORKSHOP...
REGAL?! ⁘HMPH⁘
I HOPE QUEEN CLARION HAS HER ROYAL SUN GLASSES HANDY. THERE IS SUCH A THING AS TOO BRIGHT, YOU KNOW!
AND SO, AS USUAL, TINK THROWS HERSELF INTO HER WORK...
... AND COMES UP WITH SOMETHING WONDERFUL! SHE QUICKLY FLIES OFF TO SHOW THE MINISTER OF SPRING HER LANTERN DESIGN...
THEY WOULD BE MADE WITH THE FINEST PINE CONES AND LILY PADS. IRIDESSA WILL FILL ACORN SHELLS WITH LIGHT...
HMMM...
BUT IS IT REGAL ENOUGH?
IT'S CUTE... BUT IT ISN'T REGAL ENOUGH!
⁘GULP!⁘ WHAT DO YOU SUGGEST...?
ADD SOME ROSE PETALS AND SPARKLING DEW DROPS, AND...
SLOW DOWN! I CAN'T WRITE THAT FAST!
SCRITCH
SCRATCH

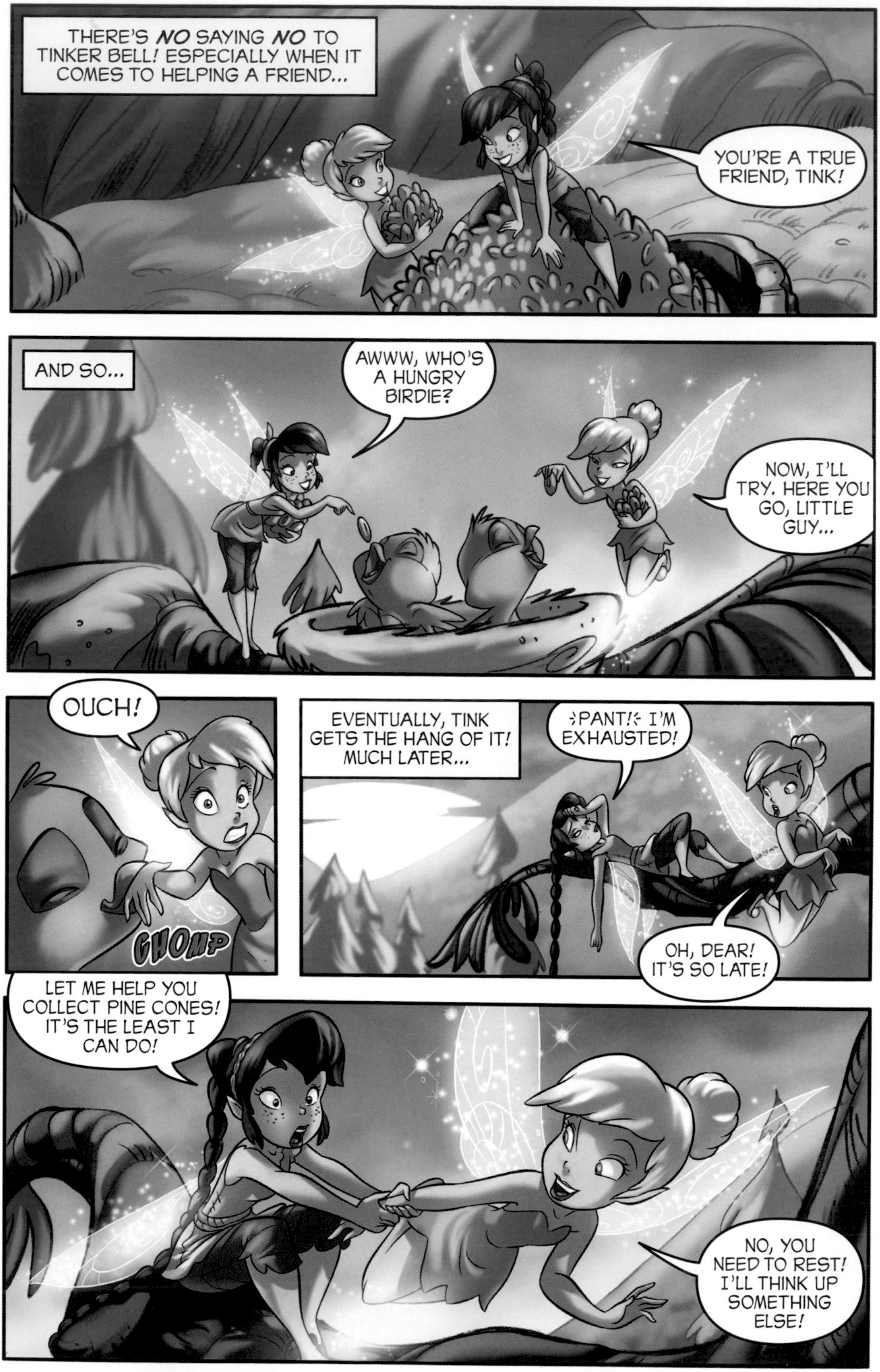

THERE'S *NO* SAYING *NO* TO TINKER BELL! ESPECIALLY WHEN IT COMES TO HELPING A FRIEND...
YOU'RE A TRUE FRIEND, TINK!
AND SO...
AWWW, WHO'S A HUNGRY BIRDIE?
NOW, I'LL TRY. HERE YOU GO, LITTLE GUY...
OUCH!
CHOMP
EVENTUALLY, TINK GETS THE HANG OF IT! MUCH LATER...
PANT! I'M EXHAUSTED!
OH, DEAR! IT'S SO LATE!
LET ME HELP YOU COLLECT PINE CONES! IT'S THE LEAST I CAN DO!
NO, YOU NEED TO REST! I'LL THINK UP SOMETHING ELSE!

- 28 -

THE END

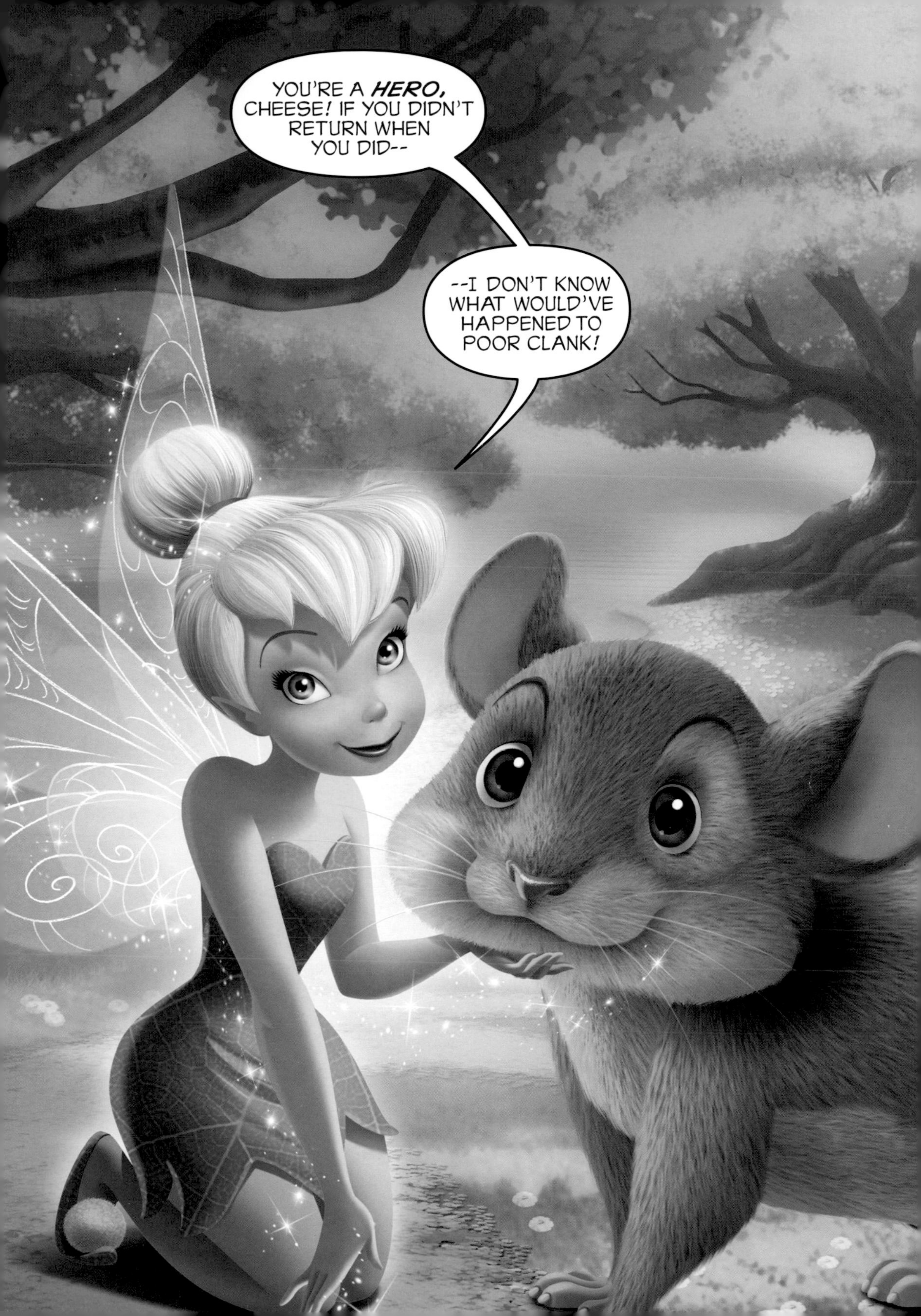
YOU'RE A ***HERO,*** CHEESE! IF YOU DIDN'T RETURN WHEN YOU DID--
--I DON'T KNOW WHAT WOULD'VE HAPPENED TO POOR CLANK!

THE MOST PRECIOUS GIFT

TINKER BELL IS NOT THE ONLY TINKER FAIRY IN PIXIE HOLLOW! THERE ARE QUITE A FEW, ACTUALLY, AND THE PLACE YOU'RE MOST LIKELY TO FIND THEM AT IS *TINKER'S NOOK...*

TODAY MARKS A VERY SPECIAL DAY FOR ONE TINKER... *CLANK,* FOR TODAY IS THE ANNIVERSARY OF HIS *ARRIVAL!*

OH, BOY, OH BOY! I WONDER WHAT MY FRIENDS ARE PLANNING...

WHY, HELLO THERE, BOBBLE? WHAT'S MY BEST FRIEND UP TO?

CLANK! THERE YOU ARE!

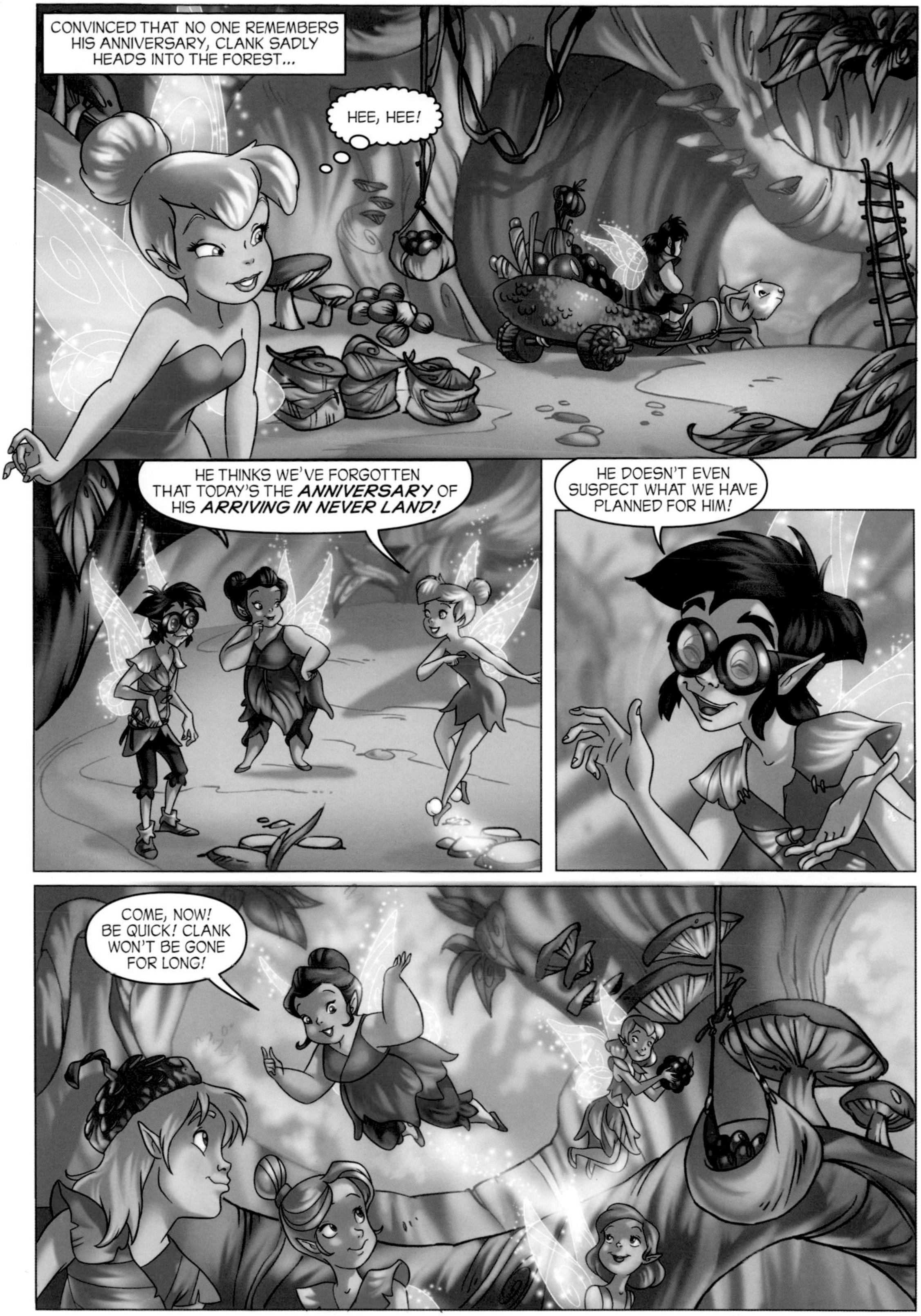
CONVINCED THAT NO ONE REMEMBERS HIS ANNIVERSARY, CLANK SADLY HEADS INTO THE FOREST...
HEE, HEE!
HE THINKS WE'VE FORGOTTEN THAT TODAY'S THE ANNIVERSARY OF HIS ARRIVING IN NEVER LAND!
HE DOESN'T EVEN SUSPECT WHAT WE HAVE PLANNED FOR HIM!
COME, NOW! BE QUICK! CLANK WON'T BE GONE FOR LONG!

- 37 -

A PRICKLY PROBLEM

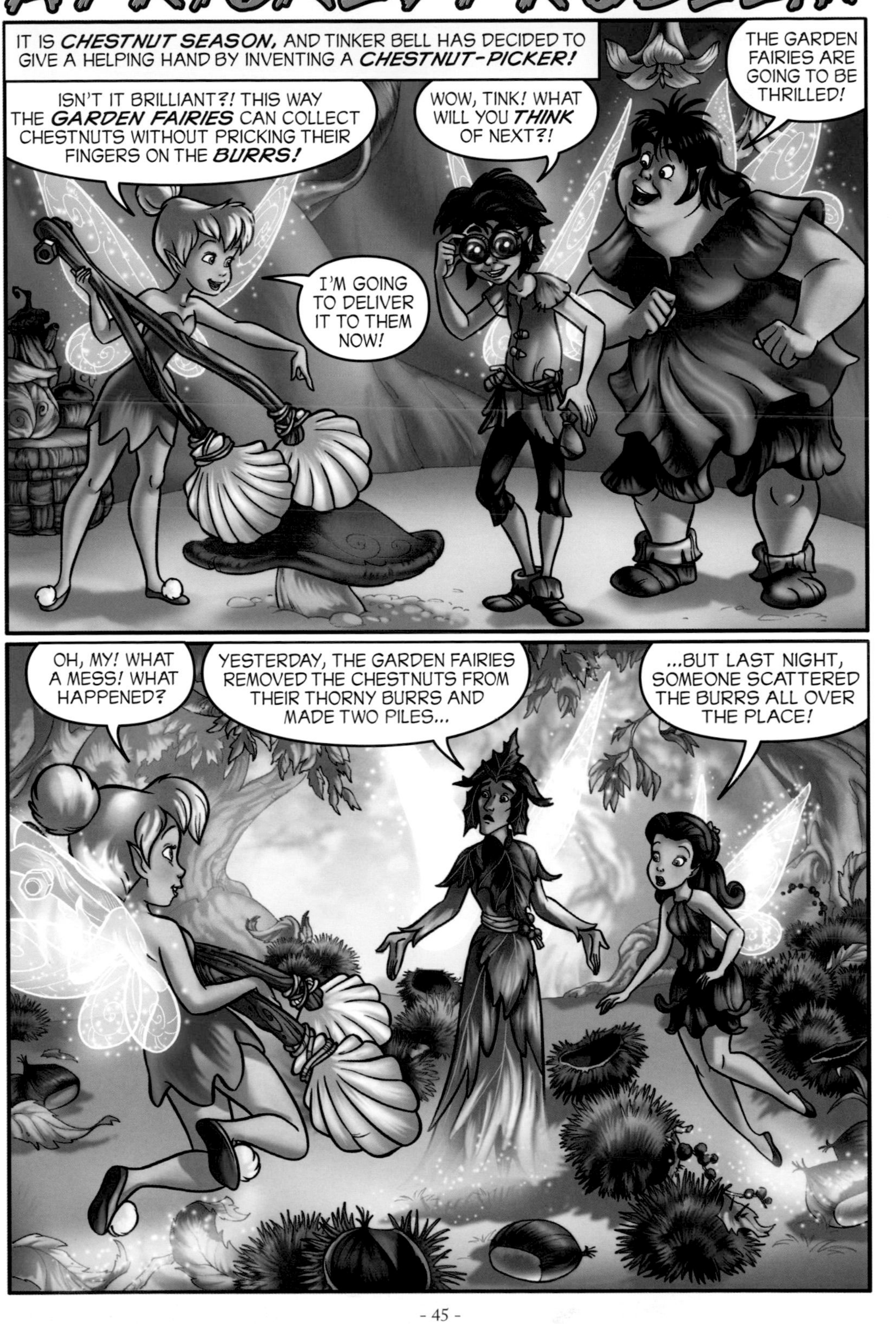
IT IS CHESTNUT SEASON, AND TINKER BELL HAS DECIDED TO GIVE A HELPING HAND BY INVENTING A CHESTNUT-PICKER!
ISN'T IT BRILLIANT?! THIS WAY THE GARDEN FAIRIES CAN COLLECT CHESTNUTS WITHOUT PRICKING THEIR FINGERS ON THE BURRS!
WOW, TINK! WHAT WILL YOU THINK OF NEXT?!
THE GARDEN FAIRIES ARE GOING TO BE THRILLED!
I'M GOING TO DELIVER IT TO THEM NOW!
OH, MY! WHAT A MESS! WHAT HAPPENED?
YESTERDAY, THE GARDEN FAIRIES REMOVED THE CHESTNUTS FROM THEIR THORNY BURRS AND MADE TWO PILES...
...BUT LAST NIGHT, SOMEONE SCATTERED THE BURRS ALL OVER THE PLACE!

THE NEXT MORNING, FAWN TRIES TO WAKE UP THEIR NEW FRIEND, BUT IT ISN'T EASY, PORCUPINES ARE *NOCTURNAL* ANIMALS. THEY SLEEP DURING THE DAY AND STAY AWAKE AT NIGHT...

C'MON, LITTLE GUY! OPEN YOUR EYES!

FINALLY, SHE TICKLES HIM AWAKE AND HE EXPLAINS EVERYTHING...

DON'T YOU WORRY, LITTLE GUY, 'CAUSE WE ARE GOING TO TAKE CARE OF IT!

OUR LITTLE FRIEND IS *LOST!* AND HE'S TOO SCARED TO GO LOOKING FOR HIS MOTHER, BROTHERS, AND SISTERS ALL ALONE.

HOW DOES THAT EXPLAIN WHY HE WAS PLAYING WITH THE CHESTNUT'S SPINY BURRS?

BECAUSE THEY *LOOK LIKE PORCUPINES!* THAT REMINDS HIM OF HOME AND MAKES HIM FEEL LESS LONELY!

THAT'S EXACTLY WHAT I THOUGHT!

WE'VE GOT TO FIND HIS FAMILY FOR HIM!

THEN WHAT ARE WE WAITING FOR?!

- 51 -

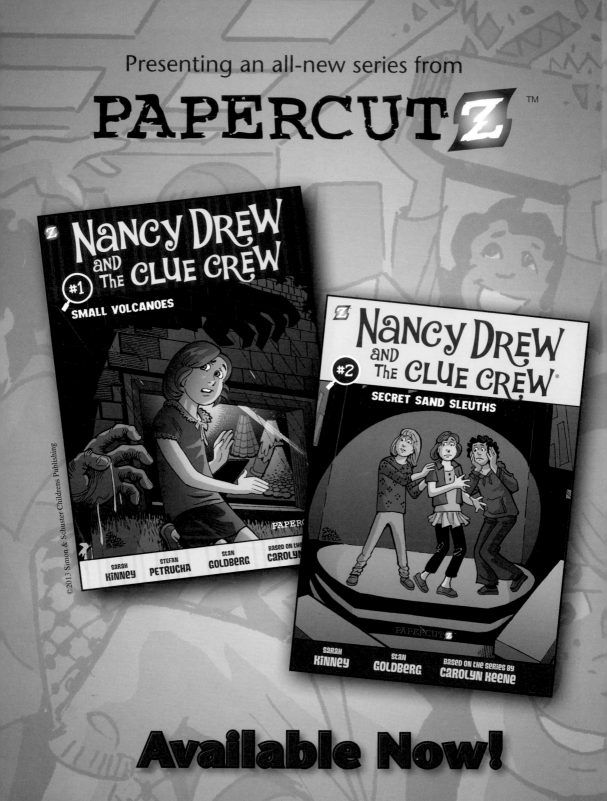

WATCH OUT FOR PAPERCUT

Welcome to the eleventh, enchanted DISNEY FAIRIES graphic novel from Papercutz, those Lost Boys and Girls dedicated to publishing great graphic novels for all ages! I'm Jim Salicrup, the Editor-in-Chief and part-time Pixie Hollow Tour Guide.

In "Where There's a Dream, There's a Way," we meet a young turtle who has a dream—she wants to fly like a fairy! I bet she just saw "Dumbo" on DVD and thought "if an elephant can fly, why, oh, why can't I?" (She might've just seen "The Wizard of Oz" too.) She was super lucky to run into Tinker Bell—if anyone can help make your dreams come true, Tink sure can!

In DISNEY FAIRIES #10, I wrote that "when I was just a child, one of my dreams was to work in comics." And like that turtle, I was super-lucky too! My dream came true when I was just fifteen, and I've been working away in comics ever since. So, I really do believe that dreams can come true, but I also know it isn't always that easy. Sometimes, you can try and try and try, and it seems like your dream is never going to come true. But if that turtle could fly, and I can work in comics, maybe your dream can come true too!

One of the countless reasons I dreamed of working in comics was to meet such amazing cartoonists as Stan Goldberg. While I haven't actually met in-person such great DISNEY FAIRIES artists as Antonello Dalena, Manuela Razzi, or Sara Storino yet, I have met Mr. Goldberg. As a kid I loved his work on MILLIE THE MODEL and CHILI from Marvel Comics, and for years he's been the top artist over at Archie Comics. Recently Stan received the National Cartoonists Society's prestigious The Gold Key award, and entered the NCS Hall of Fame. And believe it or not he's even drawing an all-new series of graphic novels for Papercutz— NANCY DREW AND THE CLUE CREW. You can even see a preview on the following pages. Having Stan Goldberg at Papercutz is not only a great honor, it's yet another dream come true!

Hey, want to help make another dream come true? Then don't miss DISNEY FAIRIES #12 "Tinker Bell and the Lost Treasure." After all, how can my dream of Papercutz becoming the most successful graphic novel publisher come true without you? And if you want your dreams to come true too, remember to keep believing in "faith, trust, and pixie dust"!

Thanks,

Jim

STAY IN TOUCH!

EMAIL: salicrup@papercutz.com
WEB: www.papercutz.com
TWITTER: @papercutzgn
FACEBOOK: PAPERCUTZGRAPHICNOVELS
REGULAR MAIL: Papercutz, 160 Broadway, Suite 700, East Wing, New York, NY 10038

Sarah Kinney – Writer   Stan Goldberg – Artist   Laurie E. Smith – Colorist   Tom Orzechowski – Letterer   Copyright © 2013 by Simon & Schuster, Inc.

Don't miss NANCY DREW AND THE CLUE CREW #2
"Secret Sand Sleuths" available at booksellers now.

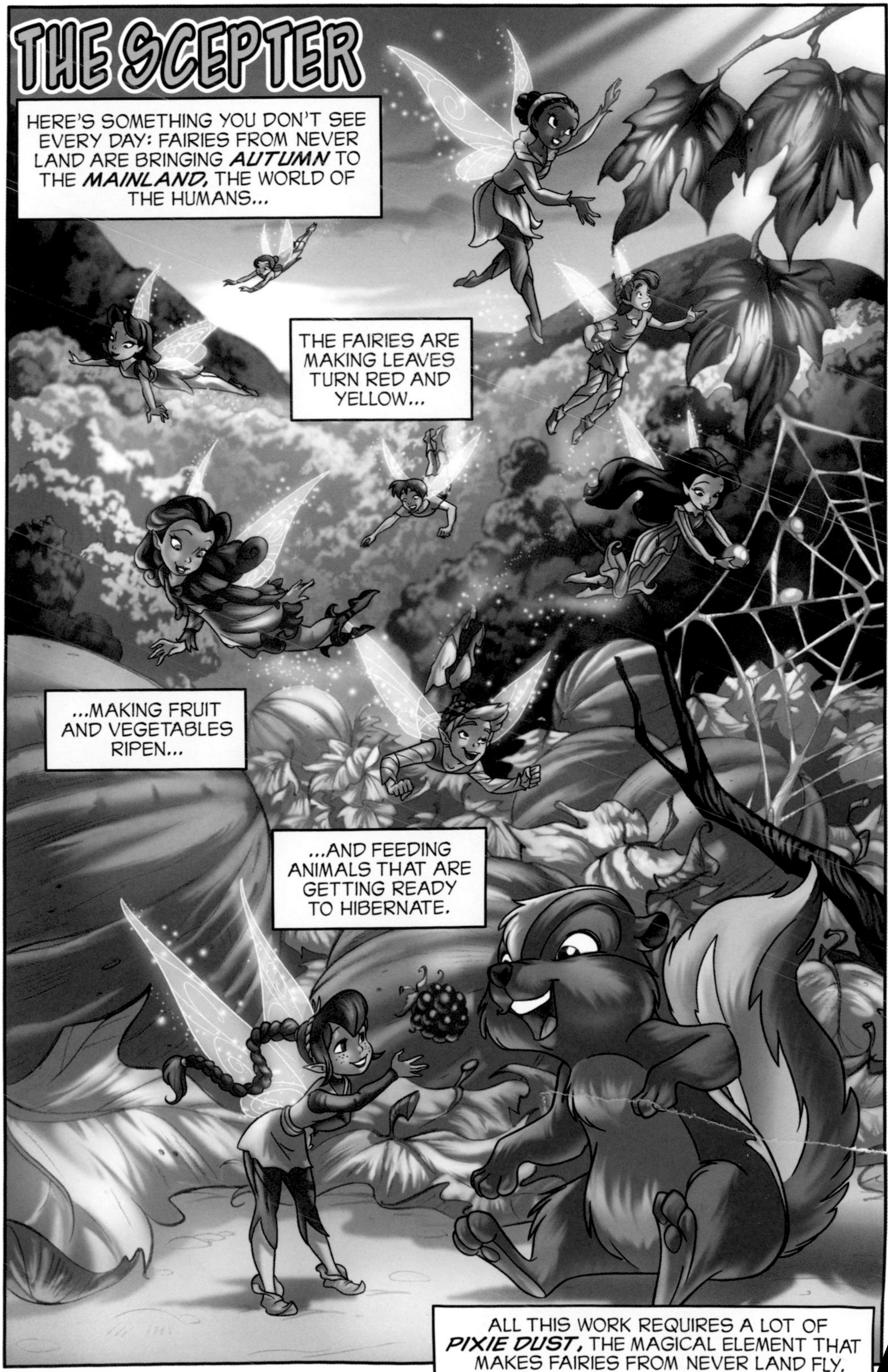
THE SCEPTER
HERE'S SOMETHING YOU DON'T SEE EVERY DAY: FAIRIES FROM NEVER LAND ARE BRINGING AUTUMN TO THE MAINLAND, THE WORLD OF THE HUMANS...
THE FAIRIES ARE MAKING LEAVES TURN RED AND YELLOW...
...MAKING FRUIT AND VEGETABLES RIPEN...
...AND FEEDING ANIMALS THAT ARE GETTING READY TO HIBERNATE.
ALL THIS WORK REQUIRES A LOT OF PIXIE DUST, THE MAGICAL ELEMENT THAT MAKES FAIRIES FROM NEVER LAND FLY.

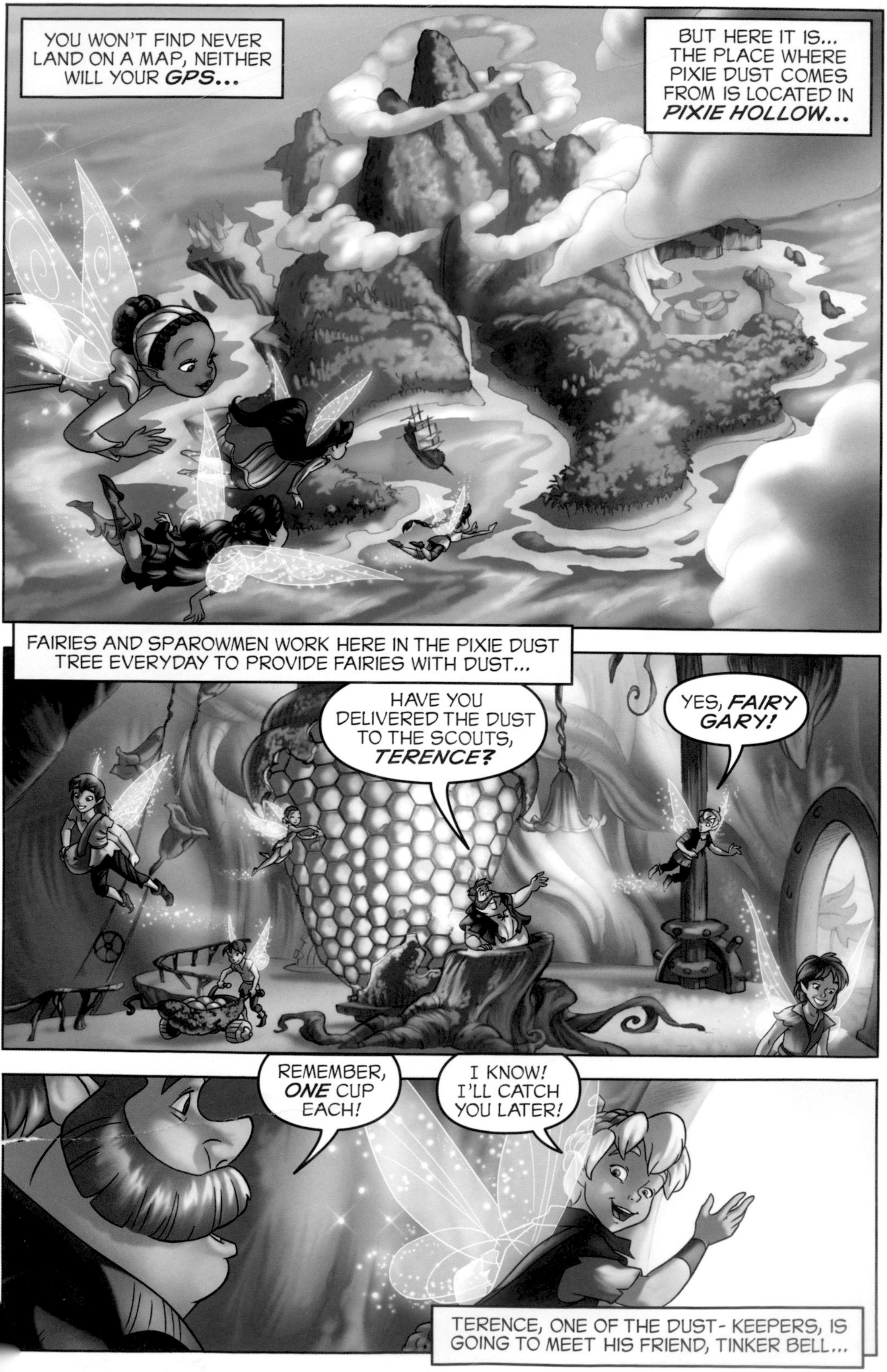
YOU WON'T FIND NEVER LAND ON A MAP, NEITHER WILL YOUR GPS...
BUT HERE IT IS... THE PLACE WHERE PIXIE DUST COMES FROM IS LOCATED IN PIXIE HOLLOW...
FAIRIES AND SPAROWMEN WORK HERE IN THE PIXIE DUST TREE EVERYDAY TO PROVIDE FAIRIES WITH DUST...
HAVE YOU DELIVERED THE DUST TO THE SCOUTS, TERENCE?
YES, FAIRY GARY!
REMEMBER, ONE CUP EACH!
I KNOW! I'LL CATCH YOU LATER!
TERENCE, ONE OF THE DUST- KEEPERS, IS GOING TO MEET HIS FRIEND, TINKER BELL...

Don't miss DISNEY FAIRIES #12 "Tinker Bell and the Lost Treasure"!

More Great Graphic Novels from PAPERCUTZ™